THE FINAL STRAW

THE FINAL STRAW

JENNY FRANCIS

Matador
9 Priory Business Park,
Wistow Road, Kibworth Beauchamp,
Leicestershire. LE8 0RX
Tel: 0116 279 2299
Email: books@troubador.co.uk
Web: www.troubador.co.uk/matador
Twitter: @matadorbooks

ISBN 978 183859 297 4

British Library Cataloguing in Publication Data.
A catalogue record for this book is available from the British Library.

Printed and bound in the UK by T J International, Padstow, Cornwall
Typeset in 11pt Minion Pro by Troubador Publishing Ltd, Leicester, UK

Matador is an imprint of Troubador Publishing Ltd

Dedicated to calling out the bullies
and making them answer for their crimes

AUTHOR'S NOTE

THE FINAL STRAW IS THE THIRD MURDER MYSTERY to feature Detective Inspector Charlie Moon and his journalist friend Jo Lyon as they team up again to unravel another case filled with unexpected twists and turns. Over two years have passed since Moon was suspended from duty for breaking house rules but the feeling his bosses are out to get him still hasn't gone away.

Like the earlier books, *The Final Straw* is set in the West Midlands at the time of the Millenium. The characters are fictional but the issues are all too real.

Jenny Francis
2020

More about books by Jenny Francis can be found at
www.meetjennyfrancis.com

PRELUDE

A HOT SUMMER DAY

AUGUST 1976

A LISTLESSNESS HUNG IN THE AIR AS THEY DROVE through the outskirts of the city making detours here and there to avoid the worst of the hold-ups. It was the start of another long hot day in the longest hottest summer anybody could ever remember. Her thoughts though were on other things as she stared out of the side window while he said nothing apart from grumbling about the heat and cursing the drivers of buses who pulled out in front.

They were almost there. A turn to the left into a quiet road where the pavements were shaded by giant horse chestnuts. She remembered those trees for many years afterwards. The way their leaves were already starting to change colour because there'd been no rain for weeks. The way they were witnesses to the moment she finally gave up hope all this could be sorted out and abandoned herself to what he told her would be best for both of them. No, the time for talking was over. Soon she'd be faced with coming to terms with what went against everything she'd ever believed in but the inner torment would have to be put to one side for now. She knew though it would come back to haunt her.

CHAPTER ONE

THE QUIET PRISONER

OCTOBER 2001

DETECTIVE INSPECTOR CHARLIE MOON REALISED he'd cut it fine. He could see the gates of the crematorium coming up ahead but it was already two minutes past two according to the digital clock on the dashboard. Fortunately for him there was a space left on the car park and, pausing only to grab his overcoat from the back seat, he hurried across to where he could see the tail end of the procession of mourners filing into the funeral chapel.

Once inside he took a seat in the empty row at the back where he had a good view of what was going on. Retired Chief Inspector Tommy Dodd had been a popular figure in the West Midlands Police so it was not surprising to see a few familiar faces from the old days had turned up to pay their respects. The escort for the coffin Moon took to be the committee of the Golf Club or else a contingent from

Tommy's Lodge who'd come to give him a good send-off. Tommy's wife had predeceased him so Moon guessed the family group down at the front consisted of his children and grandchildren.

The service was brief, just as Tommy would have wished it, then the final moment when the curtains around the coffin closed and everybody made their way out to the sounds of dance band music from the forties played through the chapel's speaker system.

Outside the autumn sunshine was still strong enough to feel pleasant as people gathered in the Garden of Remembrance to look at the flowers. Moon chatted with colleagues from days gone by who he hadn't seen for years then, just as the crowd started to disperse, he felt a soft touch on his elbow. Turning round, he saw a man in a navy-blue gabardine raincoat whose features he struggled to place at first.

'I thought I might catch you here,' the man said holding out a hand for Moon to shake.

Suddenly it clicked. Alf Stepney, formerly Detective Inspector Alf Stepney of the old West Midlands Serious Crimes Squad. A growth of stubble on his chin and a bit more flesh around his cheeks but the South Wales accent gave him away.

'How long's it been? Ten years? More? I left the Force in 1992 and, before that, I was on garden leave for twelve months.'

Moon cast his mind back. Alf Stepney survived the great purge after the Serious Crimes Squad was disbanded in 1989 but it wasn't long before he crossed swords with the new faces who came in at the top. The official version put out was he'd decided to take early retirement but it didn't take much guessing to work out he'd fallen foul of authority over something.

'How's that twat Willoughby keeping?' Stepney asked looking round and referring to Moon's boss, the Team Penda Commander. 'I didn't take a shine to him from the minute I clapped eyes on him but still that's all water under the bridge.'

Moon said nothing. He didn't know how much Stepney knew about his own clashes with Willoughby but he felt it best not to get drawn into conversation with somebody who, according to rumour, was still walking round with a chip on his shoulder.

Stepney smiled. 'Wise man Charlie. Don't talk shop with a disgruntled old bastard like me. Keep your own counsel. In this life you never know who you can trust. You must have wondered though why I decided to jack it all in when I was still a few years off picking up a full pension.'

Moon shrugged. 'We all go through moments when we think to ourselves the hassle and arse-kickings aren't worth it. I can't say I blame anybody for feeling they've had enough.'

'You don't get it, Charlie. They wanted me out. It came at the time Willoughby was still finding his feet but my guess is somebody warned him off when he mooted the idea of taking me through a disciplinary. I knew too much. I'd seen how people operated who went on to pick up their CBEs and knighthoods. I could have shopped the fucking lot of them and they knew it. Guess what? Instead of having my card marked it was just Willoughby and me in his private office and he was making me the offer I couldn't refuse.'

'They paid you off?'

'A cash lump sum, tax-free, and the offer of investment advice if I wanted it. The deal was I went quietly and signed an agreement in front of solicitors to say I'd never divulge any information about the Force or individual officers without the written consent of the Chief Constable.'

'You snatched their hands off?'

'Too true I did but the trouble is I took the money and spent the next year living it up down on the Costa del Booze. I did nothing about purchasing the annuity like I was told to do. I pissed most of it up the wall and spent the rest on slow horses and fast women – now look where I've ended up.' He unfastened his raincoat to reveal the black serge uniform he wore underneath. 'Doing security on a building site. Five twelve hour shifts: two weeks on days followed by two weeks on nights and as much overtime as I can get so I can make enough to pay the bills. You might say I've got what I deserve. I'm the biggest prat of all when you think about it.'

The last of the mourners drifted away and soon it was just the two of them left.

Stepney spoke again. 'Let me come clean, Charlie. Buttonholing you today wasn't all social. I've come with a message. Denny Wilbur wants a word. I had a phone call from one of his old associates who didn't want to be seen as a go-between. No, don't ask me what it's about because I didn't inquire. Tommy Dodd's funeral coming up today was coincidental. I reckoned it was a safe bet you'd be here and I was right.'

They walked back to the car park together.

'Let's not leave it so long next time,' Stepney said as he got into an old Vauxhall Viva with rust spots on the side. 'The years go by too quickly and none of us are getting any younger.'

• • •

Denny Wilbur was a name Charlie Moon would never forget. The brains behind the Wilbur Brothers' crime syndicate which Moon had a big hand in busting. Denny was sent down for fifteen years as an example to others although, at the time, many thought the sentence handed down by the judge was a bit harsh.

Two days passed before Moon found the time to pay a visit to Winson Green Prison where Denny was incarcerated. It was a dreary day with the rain coming down in sheets adding a further grim touch to the prison's forbidding exterior. Once inside he was taken up an echoing stairwell to a room with bare floorboards and whitewashed walls. A table and two chairs had been set up in the centre and another chair by the door. He waited. Presently he heard the sound of heavy boots coming up the stairwell. Two figures walked in: one wearing a prison officer's uniform, the other a blue boiler suit who, although he no longer sported a suntan and his face was thinner, Moon immediately recognised as the man whose collar he'd felt five years previously.

'Apologies for my appearance,' Wilbur grinned. 'You caught me in the middle of the safe-cracking classes I've been doing. They call it welding and flame-cutting in here but I'm sure you'll be pleased to see I've been giving a bit of thought to what I'm going to do when I get out.'

They sat down at the table: Moon one side, Wilbur the other. The prison officer sat on the chair by the door.

'No hard feelings Inspector,' Wilbur said resting his forearms on the table. 'I respect you did a good job for the folk of the city when you got me taken out of circulation. Let's hope one day they'll step up to the mark and give you the recognition you deserve.' He turned to the prison officer. 'Cedric, do me a favour mate and fuck off for ten minutes. There's something private I need to talk to the Inspector about.'

The prison officer looked at Moon and Moon nodded. As he went out he closed the door behind him.

'I expect you're wondering what this is about,' said Wilbur no longer with the grin on his face. 'I'd hazard a guess you thought I'd got you here so I could grass somebody up.'

'It did cross my mind.'

'In which case, sorry to disappoint you but, contrary to the view you may have formed of me during the course of our professional acquaintance, I don't fit the normal criminal profile – know what I mean? There's an altruistic side to me which surprises a lot of people. Why am I telling you this? When I came in here there was a character doing a life sentence who always walked round with a smile on his face and a Bible in his hand. At first I thought he'd gone stir-crazy. He didn't mix with anybody or say a lot and some of the callous bastards you get in places like this used to take the piss out of him. Does the name Wilson Beames mean anything to you?'

'Should it?'

'He was what some people would call a white Jamaican: everything about him was black except for the colour of his skin. He confessed to the murder of a girl back in the seventies but he didn't seem right in the head to me – you know, like he didn't belong in here. Then, one morning, they found him dead in his cell. He'd hung himself with a length of electrical cable he'd managed to get his hands on. Yes, it caused a bit of a flap at the time. Some of the staff started to get jittery because they could see the finger of blame coming round in their direction.'

'We're talking about when?'

'Back end of last year. By my reckoning he'd done over twenty years of his sentence.'

'You're saying somebody should have spotted he was in need of psychiatric care?'

'Maybe.'

'Or what?'

'He couldn't read or write yet they reckoned he'd signed a confession. Besides which he wouldn't have had the brains to know what he was signing anyway.'

'Are you suggesting he was stitched-up?'

'We all know what went on in the seventies, don't we Inspector? Some naughty people in your mob occasionally did some naughty things.'

'This was all a long time ago, Denny.'

'So what? While I may not be society's idea of a model citizen, I do know the difference between right and wrong.'

'Have you spoken to anybody else about this?'

'Not so far.'

'You singled me out? Is there a reason?'

'You come with the reputation of somebody who's prepared to get off his arse when the issues are important. Inspector, the truth is still out there somewhere. So is a killer.'

• • •

'Got a minute, Dave?'

Detective Sergeant Dave Thompson just happened to be standing by the front desk when Moon arrived back at HQ. Together they went through to Moon's office where, once the door was closed, Moon filled his young colleague in on the conversation he'd just had with Denny Wilbur.

Thompson shook his head. 'The seventies, you say. I must have been just out of nappies when all this happened. Did you buy the idea somebody like Denny Wilbur felt moved to bend your ear because his conscience won't let him sleep at night?'

'I know it stretches belief Dave but, taking Denny Wilbur out of it, I don't like the feel of this.'

'You're saying this character doing the life sentence may have been fitted-up for some reason?'

'Stranger things have happened.'

'Mr Willoughby's not going to like the idea of raking up what went on years ago particularly when he hears everything up to now hangs on the say-so of somebody like Denny Wilbur.'

Moon looked at him. 'We'll keep Mr Willoughby out of it for the time being. We'll see what this is about first.'

• • •

It was coincidence that on that same evening Moon had arranged to meet up with Jo Lyon for an after-work drink. The venue they chose was a bar in the city centre which was mainly frequented by people from nearby offices. Moon hadn't seen much of Jo over the summer so the meeting was a catch-up with what was going on in their respective worlds. Moon's relationship with Jo had landed him in hot water several times in the past. She earned her living as a freelance journalist and Willoughby had a bee in his bonnet about keeping the press at an arm's length.

The rain hadn't stopped all day and the fading light was a reminder it was only a week to go before the clocks changed. Back to winter, dark nights and coughs and colds, Moon reflected gloomily to himself as he drove along to the accompaniment of Jazz Gillum's voice and harmonica coming out of the CD player.

A shared taste in music was what brought Moon and Jo together in the first place although, over the years, their professional lives had touched many times. Jo had made her name as a campaigner on women's issues and, when Moon sat down next to her in the busy bar, she told him about the series of articles she was writing on the subject of domestic violence.

'It's difficult to assess,' she said as she watched Moon pour wine into her glass from the bottle he'd just bought at the bar. 'Is it more battered wives and girlfriends are coming forward or is something happening in society which nobody has twigged?'

'I'd put my money on the first,' Moon replied. 'In days gone by some poor woman who got knocked around every Saturday night when her husband rolled in drunk from the pub kept her mouth shut. Today it's different. Women are more inclined to speak out – which has to be a good thing.'

'So,' said Jo changing the subject. 'How's the fight against crime going. Are you and your pals making it any safer for us decent ordinary citizens to go out on the streets after dark?'

'Ask the muggers,' said Moon. 'We're too busy sitting at our desks inventing facts so people at the top can tell everybody we're meeting our targets.'

Jo smiled. 'You sound like you've had a bad day. Has somebody upset you?'

'No more than usual.'

'Anything you want to talk about? You know I'm always happy to be the listening ear.'

Moon looked at her. 'Guess who I spoke to today?'

Jo shook her head. 'Sorry you'll have to tell me. I'm no good at guessing games.'

''Denny Wilbur.'

'Not Denny Wilbur of Wilbur Brothers fame?'

'None other.' Moon then told her the story about what Birmingham's former public enemy number one had had to say about the man who hung himself in his cell after serving over twenty years of a life sentence.

Jo was shaking her head again. 'Why would anybody confess to something they didn't do?'

Moon pulled a face. 'Denny was suggesting he wasn't all there in the head.'

'Did you believe him?'

'I'm not sure,' Moon replied. 'Prisons are notorious places for gossip – some of it based on fact, some of it people spreading rumours just because they've got nothing better to do. Also Denny Wilbur isn't above trying to work some agenda of his own.'

'Like what?'

'Take your pick. Doing a favour for somebody inside or just making mischief. I wouldn't put anything past him.'

The crowd in the bar was starting to thin down. The after office hours drinkers had decided it was time to go home.

Jo spoke again. 'So where are you going to go with this?'

'I'm still thinking about it,' Moon replied holding his glass up to the light. 'Something tells me not to go rushing into anything.'

'Will you run it by Willoughby?'

'Maybe or maybe not. I'll wait and see what comes crawling out of the woodwork first.'

CHAPTER TWO

JESUS LIVES HERE

AFTER LEAVING CATHY GETTING THE GIRLS READY for school, Moon's first call of the day was a visit to the dentist – an event he wasn't looking forward to even though it was just for a check-up. It was the morning after his get-together with Jo.

Thankful when the ordeal of sitting in the dentist's chair for twenty minutes was over, he did the remaining few miles to HQ in light mid-morning traffic. It was just after eleven when he arrived.

'Morning,' said Sergeant Hobbs who was on front desk duty.

Moon passed through to his office, stopping off at the kitchen to grab a cup of coffee. On the way in he'd noticed Willoughby's car parked in its usual place with Detective Inspector Millership's next to it. There was a rumour doing the rounds Millership was in for a promotion soon, something which would come as no surprise to Moon who'd kept a watchful eye on the career of his upwardly mobile colleague ever since he appeared on the scene. The thought of Willoughby and Millership with their heads locked together in one of the upstairs conference rooms cast Moon's mind back to February and the blast he'd been given for failing to keep Willoughby informed. Willoughby had made it abundantly clear there'd be big trouble if there were any more instances of Moon not communicating in the way he'd been told to do but here he was now with the potentially explosive material which had come his way just twenty-four hours earlier courtesy of Denny Wilbur. Moon sighed.

'Can I have a word Guv?' It was Thompson who'd put his head round the door – Thompson who'd been charged with the job of finding out what he could about the Wilson Beames' case without causing a stir.

'This murder we're talking about happened in July 1978,' Thompson began leaning his tall frame against the filing cabinet. 'A girl named Sharon Baxter found by a canal with multiple stab wounds. Beames was sentenced at Birmingham Crown Court later the same year. Criminal records showed he had no previous convictions. His date of birth was given as 19.03.1952 so he was twenty-six at the time. If the information about him hanging himself late last year is correct, he would have been forty-eight meaning he'd spent nearly half of his life in prison.'

'There was no appeal against the conviction?'

'Apparently not. Beames confessed to the murder but otherwise the information is scrappy.'

'What do you mean by scrappy?'

Thompson took a deep breath. 'All the files on the case have gone missing. The witness statements, the forensic evidence, the lot – it's all vanished. Nothing left on the shelves except empty boxes.'

'We've been here before, Dave.'

'I know Guv.'

'What do we know about the girl?'

'She was eighteen, a student at the University with her family home somewhere in South Yorkshire.'

'How do we know this?'

Thompson smiled. 'I used my initiative and went round to the public library. It took a bit of sifting through old newspapers but I found a few items which made interesting reading.' He handed over a sheaf of photocopies stapled together at the corner. Moon thumbed through them seeing straight away they consisted of press clippings going back to the discovery of the girl's body and ending with Beames' sentencing.

'Shall I leave those with you?' Thompson asked.

'Please,' said Moon.

'Don't forget it's Scotty's birthday,' said Thompson referring to Detective Constable Scott who had recently distinguished himself by breaking two of his fingers in a car door. 'We're going to the pub at lunchtime and I assume you still want to come along.'

'Providing I'm not expected to pick up the tab,' Moon replied with a smile on his face.

After Thompson went, Moon settled back to cast his eye through the newspaper cuttings in more detail. One of the first he came to was a report of Beames' arrest describing him as a hospital porter. There was an interview with the victim's parents and a grainy photograph of them standing in what looked like their front garden. The piece ended with comments from some civic dignitary of the time about making the streets safer by cracking down on people carrying knives. What struck Moon most of all though was the pace at which events must have moved. From what he could see only a few days lapsed between the discovery of the girl's body and Beames' arrest. The police had been quick to catch their man and no doubt the officers concerned received a few pats on the back for their good work.

• • •

Moon arrived at the pub shortly after one: Scott with his fingers in splints and a hard-done by look on his face, his partner Detective Constable Tamberlin getting in the pints while Moon and Thompson settled for halves. The talk was about the prospect of Scott not making a full recovery from his injuries and how, at a push, it might put him in line for an early retirement pension on medical grounds.

'Do me a favour,' said Scott starting to take the leg-pulling seriously.

After twenty minutes of listening to the banter, Moon made an excuse and left but, instead of driving back to the office, he took the short trip to one of his regular haunts when he needed space to think – a piece of derelict land overlooking the railway lines which went in and out of the city.

Moon's misspent youth as a train-spotter was partly the reason why he was drawn to this place where, at this time of year, the willow herbs had gone to seed so everywhere was a mass of silky grey plumes. The sun was doing its best to come out and it felt warm enough to sit with the window down. After five minutes he took his phone out of his pocket and tapped in a string of numbers he knew from memory. He waited for the line to connect then, after three rings, Jo's voice answered.

'Can you speak?'

'If it's quick,' Jo replied.

Moon then filled her in on Thompson's discovery that everything to do with the case of Wilson Beames had mysteriously gone missing from the archives.

'It's not the first time it's happened,' Moon added. 'It could be negligence or it could point the finger at somebody trying to do away with evidence they didn't want coming back to haunt them.'

'Like who?'

'Police officers with something they wanted to hide. The same people hanging a murder charge on a man who was completely innocent.'

'But why would they do that?'

'Your guess is as good as mine.'

'So how can I help?'

'Dave Thompson dug out some old newspaper reports covering the trial and reading them gave me an idea. Somebody from the press might be able to throw some light on what happened in court back in 1978. Somebody who was there.'

'That's why you're asking me?'

'Once this goes official I'm guessing a lot of people will be trying to cover their backs. I want to get a head start on them.'

'Charlie, in 1978 I was a junior typist working for the Birmingham Post and Mail. I didn't do crime reporting. I never have done.'

'I didn't mean you. I was pinning my hopes on you knowing somebody.'

'1978 was a long time ago.'

'I know.'

'Look Charlie, leave it with me but understand I'm not making any promises. A few of the names that spring to mind have passed away. I'll try making some phone calls but I can't say I'm over-optimistic about the outcome.'

'Thanks Jo, you're a star.'

• • •

Driving to the office the following day, Moon flicked on the radio to catch the weather report. A ridge of high pressure was building up over the country so the forecast was for light winds and no rain.

After talking it over with Thompson, Moon decided to bring Scott and Tamberlin in on the task of putting out some feelers to try and find out more on the quiet about what happened in 1978. The four of them were now gathered in the cramped space of Moon's office where the two young DCs listened in silence to what he had to say.

'Need I remind you we're going back to the days of the Serious Crimes Squad,' Moon added. 'Things went on which shouldn't have gone on.'

Tamberlin looked up. 'Any idea who led the investigation into the girl's murder?'

'Not yet. The likelihood is somebody who's now retired or passed away.'

'You're thinking along the lines we could be looking at some kind of conspiracy to pervert the course of justice?'

'I'm thinking nothing. There were some bad apples in the Serious Crimes Squad but don't run away with the idea everybody was tarred with the same brush.'

Scott spoke next. 'What you've not said Boss is whether the victim was acquainted with the bloke who hung himself.'

'Again we don't know Scotty but I can see where you're coming from because it's a question I keep asking myself. Why did the police pull in Beames so quickly? If he had no connection with the girl why did they pick on him?'

Thompson chipped in. 'You could understand it if Beames had a record but he didn't. He must have been on the radar for some other reason.'

'Was there a suggestion he had mental problems?' Tamberlin offered. 'If so, perhaps he was on the watch list because somebody saw he might have dangerous tendencies.'

'Well one thing's for certain,' said Moon stretching his arms. 'We won't find out anything by sitting here floating theories around the table. Tambo, you and Scotty could make yourselves useful by chatting to a few old lags who've done time in Winson Green. See if anybody knows anything which would lend weight or otherwise to Denny Wilbur's version of events. As for Beames, we know he worked at a hospital and there's the address on his crime sheet where he was living at the time of his arrest.'

'Do you want me to pop round and knock on the door?' This came from Thompson. 'Somebody may still be living there who can give us some information.'

'No Dave. I'll do it. I can't let the chance to get out of this place for a couple of hours slip by.'

• • •

It was just after three in the afternoon when Moon left the office. His destination was a district of the city which had once been the home to foundries, forges and rolling mills but where decades of decline and recession had left their scars. The sun was dipping in a clear blue sky criss-crossed with jet contrails as he parked his car next to a builder's skip in a street of Victorian terraced houses where he scanned the numbers on the doors to find the one he was looking for. Number twenty-five was on the side of the street in shadow with nothing to distinguish it from the rest of the properties except for a wooden plaque screwed to the wall. There was a few feet of frontage behind a privet hedge scarcely big enough to be called a garden but it was the plaque which caught Moon's eye as he drew close enough to read it. An oval cut out of plywood on which somebody had stencilled the simple message 'Jesus lives here'.

A woman answered the door – a woman in her late thirties or early forties with Afro-Caribbean features and light coloured skin reminding Moon of Denny Wilbur's description of Wilson Beames. A white Jamaican: Moon held up his ID for her to inspect.

'I'm looking for the family of a former inmate of Winson Green Prison,' he said. 'I need help with an investigation.'

'You must mean my brother,' the woman replied pulling her cardigan round her shoulders.

'It may be better if I came in,' Moon said casting his eyes up and down the street.

The woman nodded and turned around. Inside there was a narrow hallway where Moon wiped his feet on the doormat before following her through to the front room. There, sitting in an armchair, was another much older woman who looked up as Moon entered.

'This is my mother,' the younger woman said.

There was a gas fire which didn't give out much heat and, on the walls, framed pictures of what looked like scenes from the New Testament and a sampler somebody had made with a verse from the scriptures.

The younger woman spoke, raising her voice in the manner of one addressing somebody hard of hearing. 'This gentleman wants to ask some questions about Wilson.'

The older woman smiled and looked across at Moon. 'Have you come from the prison?' she asked.

'No mother,' her daughter said. 'The Inspector is from the police.'

'Police?' The mother looked confused. 'Wilson hasn't done anything wrong because his soul is up in Heaven where the Good Lord is looking after him.'

'I'm sorry to have to talk to you about events you must find painful,' Moon said.

'You must be mistaken Mr Policeman. I'm not in pain. If I was I would go and see the doctor.'

The younger woman caught Moon's eye. 'It's time for mother's rest,' she said and, indicating to Moon to follow her, she led him back into the hallway then through a kitchen and out into the back yard.

'Mother's mind is slipping away,' she said. 'Some days are better than others but perhaps it's better she forgets.'

The yard was a little suntrap with a slabbed patio and a neatly tended vegetable patch while a tomato vine grew up a trellis on one wall from which hung the last of the summer crop still ripening. There were two plastic chairs with cushions on them where the woman indicated they should sit.

'I was still at school when Wilson was sent to prison,' she said. 'I stayed with Mother because, with Wilson gone, she didn't have anybody to look after her.'

'Your mother's widowed?'

'My father went off when I was a little girl. He was a white man. The last we heard of him, he was living in Liverpool.'

'It sounds like your mother has had a hard life.'

'She found work where she could get it. Cleaning offices, working part-time in factories, sometimes two or three jobs at the same time. She had her faith to keep her going.'

'Your brother hanging himself must have come as a terrible shock.'

She smiled. 'Mother accepted it as God's will. People came from the prison and one of them offered her counselling but Mother never shared her grief. Still, Inspector, you've not come here to listen to our troubles. Something else has brought you today.'

'Earlier this week I paid a visit to the prison because one of the inmates there asked to see me. He knew your brother. He told me he was an innocent man, the victim of a miscarriage of justice, and I'm trying to find out if he's telling me the truth or not.'

The woman stiffened. 'I was thirteen when they took Wilson away. I'd just got back from school when the police came knocking on the door. Wilson was doing nights at the hospital so he was still in bed but it didn't stop them going up the stairs and putting the handcuffs on him. They didn't even give him chance to change out of his pyjamas.'

'Did Wilson know the girl who was found murdered?'

'She wasn't from round here. Somebody told us later she was from up North.'

'I'm told she was stabbed. Do you know if it was Wilson's habit to carry a knife?'

The woman shook her head. 'Wilson was a gentle boy. Never got into fights. Didn't have anything to do with gangs. When he wasn't at work he spent most of his time at home. The garden was his passion. He grew all sorts of things, here and down at the allotment he rented off the Council. After he went to prison Mother and I did our best to keep everything going. Now it's just me.'

'He confessed to the murder. Why did he do that?'

'Like I said, Inspector, I was only thirteen. I know they kept him down at the police station for hours.'

'And what…?'

'It didn't take Wilson long to get confused. He struggled at school and Mother always said I was the one with all the brains. He was supposed to have signed something but Wilson had never been able to write his own name so the policemen weren't telling the truth.'

'Why do you think the police picked on your brother?'

'Wilson was always known for going round with a big smile on his face. It was why he was so popular with the staff and patients at the hospital. He smiled at everybody including this white woman who moved in down the street. The next thing we knew a policeman came knocking on the door accusing Wilson of sexually harassing her. Wilson kept a civil tongue in his head in the way he was brought up to do but he told the policeman he'd never spoken to the woman so he couldn't see what the fuss was about. The policeman then got shirty with him and all this went on outside the front door so I heard every word. The policeman said a lot of bad things to Wilson – race things – and Wilson was truly upset about it but Mother told him to turn the other cheek in a Christian way. A long time after we learned the policeman's car was regularly seen parked outside the woman's house.'

'You don't know the policeman's name?'

'If I did, I've forgotten it. Besides he hasn't been seen round here for years and the white woman disappeared soon after all this happened.'

'In time terms, when are we talking about? How long was it between the incident with the policeman and Wilson being arrested?'

'Weeks rather than months. Again it's hard to remember especially when it's something you've always done your best to forget.'

'Did Wilson mention the brush with the policeman to his solicitor?'

'Nothing about what happened back then was said in front of me so I don't know the answer to your question. In this house some things weren't felt fit for a child's ears.'

'Did your mother and you visit Wilson in prison?'

'As often as we could.'

'How did he seem?'

'His usual self. Cheerful.'

'Did he ever complain about the way he was being treated.'

'No, never. He was full of praise for everybody. After his death Mother and I received a lot of kind letters from people – staff and prisoners. They all thought a lot of him.'

'Did he ever talk about what happened in 1978?'

'It was a subject he never discussed.'

'Before his death, did you ever get the feeling he might be drawn to self-harm?'

'Again no but Wilson was always a closed book. You never knew what was going on inside his head.'

As Moon went out he passed the door to the front room where he caught a glimpse of the old woman asleep in her chair.

'How far is it to where the girl's body was found?' he asked Beames' sister as he took his leave of her.

'Down by the canal,' she replied and gave him directions. 'It's not a place I go to myself but people tell me it's not changed.'

Back at the car Moon sat for a while watching the comings and goings in the street. A group of Asian kids came past carrying a cricket bat. A man stood on the corner smoking a cigarette. His eyes drifted back to the house with the plaque on the door. He imagined the scene all those years ago: police cars drawn up then a frightened man in his pyjamas with a blanket thrown over his shoulders being dragged across the pavement while the neighbours looked on. Moon grimaced. There was a stench of rottenness in the air. A stench he knew all too well.

• • •

Ten minutes later he was making a right turn off a busy High Street into a narrow side road so hidden between a row of shops he almost missed it. The road took him past a derelict factory with its insides gutted out before crossing over a bridge spanning a railway line and a canal. A few yards past the bridge he drew up on to a piece of spare land. Further on there was what looked like a scrapyard and, beyond that, the road came to an abrupt end.

Getting out of the car the nip in the air struck him immediately now the sun had gone down. He walked back to the bridge noticing the stillness as he did. Pausing to peer over the parapets, he saw how the railway and the canal followed a deep cutting which went off in both directions as far as the eye could see. A mist was coming up off the water of the canal slowly wrapping itself wraith-like around the bridge's sandstone pillars. A train went by, its cantilevers showering sparks from the overhead wires. Was it here where the girl's body was found? On the lonely towpath down below or somewhere among the tangle of weeds and bushes which grew on both sides of the cutting? Moon looked for a way down but he couldn't see one. Fences with spiked pales had been erected to keep out trespassers but it was possible they may not have been there twenty-three years ago. Twenty-three years ago the place would have been crawling with forensic officers looking for clues but now there was nobody. As the first few stars came out, he made his way slowly back to the car. The stench of rottenness had come back.

CHAPTER THREE

SPENCER MIDDLEWEEK

A FEW DAYS PASSED BEFORE MOON MANAGED TO catch up with Doctor Lionel Moet, the be-all and end-all of forensic pathology in the West Midlands – a figure of eminence who had been on the scene for as far back as anybody could remember. Nell, as he was better known to his close associates, had been attending a symposium in London and Moon met him at six in the bar of a hotel near New Street station where he had just arrived on the early evening train. The bar was a well-known haunt of serious drinkers and Moon guessed Nell was one of its regular patrons.

'Cheers,' said Nell raising the tumbler of single malt Moon had put in front of him. Rumours Nell had been told to cut down on his alcohol intake had been circulating for some time so Moon hazarded a guess this was his first of the day. Moon stuck to a tomato juice using the excuse he still had work to do back at the office.

'Glad to know the boys in blue are hard at it,' said Nell nodding his head to somebody he recognised. 'Nine parts of it is bullshit, I expect. No offence to you, Charlie. So what's new? I'm sure you've not collared me at this hour just to talk about this and that.'

'I want you to cast your mind back,' said Moon drawing his chair closer. 'Twenty-three years ago. The murder of a girl in her teens named Sharon Baxter. Multiple stab wounds. Does it ring any bells?'

Nell put his tumbler down. 'A white girl who came from Yorkshire. Student at the University if I remember correctly. You never forget the young ones, Charlie. She was a good-looker, a blonde with a pretty face. It was her father who made the trip from Sheffield to identify the body. Have you read the post-mortem report I wrote?'

'It's vanished along with everything else to do with the case. I was banking on your memory helping me fill in the missing pieces.'

'She was attacked with a knife. The murder weapon was never found. She'd been stabbed several times all the way from the pubic area to just under the ribcage. At first we couldn't work out why but then we discovered she was pregnant – ten to twelve weeks gone.'

'Are you saying somebody was trying to do away with her and the child she was carrying?'

'Put whatever interpretation on it you like but that was the way it looked to me. Some peculiar form of gratification – sexual perhaps. Who knows what turns these people on?

'It would not have been obvious she was pregnant?'

'Not to somebody walking past her in the street.'

'Which seems to suggest the killer knew her or, at least, knew she was pregnant.'

'I was told the man who confessed worked at the hospital. It's possible he may have come into contact with her there. What's certain though was he wasn't the father of the child. We did tests. Now, Charlie, it's your turn to tell me what all this is about. I'm guessing something's surfaced which has thrown everything back in the melting pot.'

Moon took the next ten minutes filling him in. When he finished speaking, Nell sat for a while running his finger around the top of his tumbler.

Moon broke the silence. 'The senior police officer in charge of the investigation – do you recall his name?'

'A lot of faces came and went at the time. I've got some old diaries I've kept which might help jog my memory. They're in a box at the office. Charlie, is this taking us back to the bad old days?'

'It could be, Nell. I wish it wasn't but so far the signs aren't good.'

• • •

Out on the streets, the fog that had been hanging around all day was starting to turn into a pea-souper. Moon saw Nell off in a taxi then made his way back to the multi-storey where he'd left the car. The fog deadened the noise of the traffic and filtered out the brightness of the street lights giving everywhere a strange and unfamiliar look. Reaching the entrance to the car park, his footsteps echoed as he made his way up to the second level by way of a concrete stairwell which stank of stale urine. The car stood practically alone in acres of space vacated by shoppers and office workers who'd gone home long ago. The only light came from grimy bulkhead lamps fixed to the low ceiling while the fog seeped up from the streets through the car park's open sides. No sound apart from the occasional screech of tyres, he looked around to make sure nobody was lurking in the shadows as he fed coins one by one into the ticket machine. For Charlie Moon, the feeling of being watched had never gone away.

· · ·

Next morning the fog was slow to lift as he set out from home. A hazy sun struggled to break through as he drove along the dual carriageway while there was news on the radio of a serious pile-up on the motorway.

He'd not been in the office long when the call from Jo came through.

'Charlie, I'm sorry I've not been back to you sooner but tracking down the people I wanted to speak to proved harder than I thought. Does the name Spencer Middleweek mean anything to you?'

'Should it?'

'He worked as a crime reporter on a few of the local papers in the sixties and seventies before moving down to Fleet Street. Nobody had heard of him for years and several of the people I contacted thought he'd passed away. He retired about fifteen years ago and went to live in Oxfordshire but from there he completely vanished until he surfaced recently in a private residential home in Great Malvern. How he came to be there isn't clear.'

'He sounds like he could be worth talking to. What would we have to do to set up a meeting?'

'I'm not sure. I remember he wasn't a great fan of the police so how he'd feel about sharing memories with you could go one way or the other. I'll see what I can do but, again, I make no promises.'

• • •

The catch up session with Thompson, Scott and Tamberlin had been slotted in for eleven to give Scott time to visit the outpatients' department at the hospital to have his fingers checked over. They crowded into Moon's office again where the first item on the agenda was an ongoing investigation into a gang of Yardies who had moved up from London three months previously. There were numerous tip-offs about what the Yardies were up to but so far nothing substantial had come to light.

When the discussion about the Yardies finished Moon took the opportunity to fill everybody in on his conversation with Wilson Beames' sister and what Nell Moet had had to say about the post-mortem examination he carried out in 1978.

'Should we be focussing on the race aspect to this?' said Thompson. 'If Beames' sister is to be believed this started with a policeman not liking the idea of a black man eyeing up his bit of tom. It doesn't take a big stretch of the imagination to work out how the same policeman would have reacted if the word went out a) a white girl had been knifed down by the canal and b) to pull in any weirdos who lived on the patch.'

'With a dangerous killer loose on the streets I can see the police being under pressure to make an arrest,' Moon said. 'Some of the niceties may have got overlooked in the rush to find somebody who fitted the profile of the man they were after.'

'Guv.' This came from Tamberlin. 'Let's not rule out the possibility the police knew the identity of the killer. They realised Beames wasn't the sharpest tool in the box so he presented them with the perfect candidate to hang the girl's murder on. The real culprit was somebody they wanted to protect.'

'You mean like an informer?' said Scott

'Or some big nob. Or one of them.'

'Which brings us back to the girl being pregnant,' said Moon. 'We know Beames wasn't the father but it begs the question who was? Was it somebody who got the girl in the family way then panicked? Was he already married or was he frightened what his parents might say or didn't he want to be saddled with the bills – the list goes on but did he see the easy way out of the mess he'd got himself in was to do away with her?'

'Sounds a bit extreme to me,' said Scott looking doubtful. 'Why not just go and get an abortion? Was it legal in 1978?'

'The law changed in the sixties,' Moon replied. 'But that doesn't rule out the girl having her own ideas about taking the life of an unborn child – which, in turn, could give us a motive.'

'You mean they had a fight over it?' said Scott. 'He wanted her to have an abortion but she refused?'

'Something on those lines but, without knowing what was going on in her life, we're fishing in the dark.'

• • •

The Elms Nursing Home was situated in a quiet crescent of nineteenth century villas in the faded elegance of the spa town of Great Malvern. Almost a week had gone by since Moon had last spoken to Jo then the phone call came through to say she'd managed to fix up a meeting with Spencer Middleweek thanks to an old contact pulling a few strings.

'He's agreed to speak to you subject to me being present,' she explained to Moon as they drove down the motorway on a day which threatened rain. 'Like I said he doesn't trust policemen. He thinks seventy per cent of them are up to no good and the ones that aren't are too thick to know the difference.'

Moon smiled. As a precaution he'd booked a day's leave so he didn't have to account to anybody about where he was going or who he was going to see.

The Elms had a few parking spaces for visitors on a gravelled area at the front. There was a damp smell of autumn in the air as they got out of the car next to a heap of leaves somebody had raked up. The front door was at the top of a short flight of steps with a ramp at the side to give wheelchair access. Jo pressed the button to the intercom and a woman's voice answered.

Once inside they were met by a receptionist who confirmed they were 'expected'. Moon looked round. The place had a faded look with wallpaper taken straight from an early sixties pattern book. There was a smell of dinners and incontinence.

'We've put Mr Middleweek in the Green Room,' the receptionist explained. 'You'll find nobody disturbs you there.'

Jo thanked her and they followed the directions she gave which took them along a corridor where dark prints of rural scenes hung on the walls. Through an open doorway Moon caught a glimpse of old dears sitting around in armchairs while women in pink overalls served them with tea.

The Green Room had a metal plate screwed to the door to confirm they were in the right place. Inside they saw straight away the figure on the far side sitting in a high-backed chair wearing a dressing gown over a pair of pyjamas and slippers on his feet.

'Sorry for the attire,' he said. 'It's a case of take me as you find me. One doesn't get the couture in places like this.'

Jo introduced herself. 'I've read some of your articles,' he smiled. 'The press needs more people like you to unearth the wickedness that goes on in this world we live in.' He turned his eyes to Moon. 'I take it this is your rozzer friend. He doesn't look a bad fellow but you can never tell from first impressions. By the way, forgive me if I have to have a drag on this.' He pointed to a bottle of oxygen with a mask at the end of a plastic tube which was standing on the floor at the side of his chair. 'Fucked up my respiratory system years ago thanks to eighty fags a day. All my own stupid fault. Still, it's too late for regrets now.'

Moon studied his features. Face scored with wrinkles, hair tousled and in need of a cut, blue eyes sharp as needles – he looked to be in his early eighties.

One of the pink overalled women came in carrying a tray with tea things on it and a plate of assorted biscuits.

'You're an angel Gladys,' said Middleweek with a sly grin on his face. 'Now be an even bigger angel and play mother for us.'

The woman was smiling. 'What did your last slave die of?' she said in a gentle country accent as she poured the tea. 'My old dad always used to say soft-soapers like you had linings of silver stuck onto the insides of their mouths.'

Jo waited for Gladys to leave before she broached the subject of their visit. Middleweek listened attentively, occasionally dunking a biscuit in his tea and interrupting only to ask questions when he felt something needed clarifying.

'A lot of pieces are starting to fit into place,' he said putting his teacup down on a small table at the side of his chair. 'You weren't around in the seventies, I suppose. The name Toby Ankerdine won't mean anything to you.'

'It rings a faint bell,' said Moon.

'Toby Ankerdine was one of the partners in the law firm of Ankerdine, Redmarley and Rolfe – now defunct, I understand. He represented your man Beames in court. I was there and watched him perform.'

'He didn't do a good job?'

Middleweek laughed. 'It was more than that. Toby Ankerdine couldn't stand the sight of black men. He made no secret of it.'

'Did you cover the trial?' This came from Jo.

'What there was of it. The chappie in the dock hardly spoke a word apart from confirming his name and address and pleading guilty. He stood there between two coppers looking like he didn't have a clue what was going on. When it was over, there was the usual hue and cry about bringing back the death penalty. It's a tragic irony the poor sod ended up hanging himself.'

'What were the whispers doing the rounds at the time?' Moon asked.

'Nobody spoke up for the black guy that was for sure. Nobody painted signs on the walls saying Beames is innocent. Nobody did anything apart from heaping praise on the police for bringing a dangerous criminal to justice.'

'What about you? What did you think?'

'My views of the police have mellowed since back in those days, Inspector. Yes, it did cross my mind your man had been browbeaten into signing a confession somebody put in front of him. When I saw Toby Ankerdine was the person who'd been put there to fight his corner, my suspicions doubled.'

'You thought it was a stitch-up?'

'I thought all sorts of things.'

'Such as?'

'At first I thought it was driven by race. Some nasty bunch of bastards in your lot stoking up a racist agenda by parading a black man in front of everybody and accusing him of butchering to death a nice middle class white girl. Yes, it played well to the public gallery. You could hear the whispers of 'Animal' and 'Put him behind bars where he belongs' all along the back row.'

'Did you change your mind about the racist agenda?' said Jo.

Middleweek studied her face thoughtfully. 'I started to see there must be more to it. Senior police officers and people like Toby Ankerdine wouldn't put their careers on the line just for the sake of getting a black man sent to prison. Besides, in terms of any racist feeling the case stirred up, the impact was short-lived. Six months down the line everybody had forgotten about it.'

'So, if it wasn't race, what was it about?'

'Your guess is as good as mine. The police closed ranks as they always do when they're trying to hide the truth. Why did Toby Ankerdine play along with them? It's a question I've asked myself a number of times over the years. Did they have something on him or was he fishing for a favour in return? You can come up with any number of possible explanations.'

'Can you back any of this up?' Moon asked watching Middleweek as he put the oxygen mask to his face and took a deep breath.

Middleweek shook his head. 'Sadly no, Inspector. I put Birmingham behind me when I moved down to the Smoke. I often thought about your fellow languishing in his cell and wondered was what going through his head.'

As Jo and Moon took their leave of him, Middleweek stood up to shake hands. 'A word of warning from an old hack, Inspector – fighting injustice is not for the faint-hearted especially when you're up against the forces of the Establishment. Never underestimate what they're capable of doing when it comes to looking after one of their own. Watch your back.'

CHAPTER FOUR

JIM BAXTER

MOON LEFT THE HOUSE WITH A REMINDER FROM
Cathy to call at the fancy dress hire shop to collect the
girls' costumes for the school Hallowe'en party. It was the
first Monday after the clocks changed. An extra hour in
bed over the weekend for some of those who stood at the
bus stops or sat in the traffic tailbacks while Moon spent
the journey listening to the radio to catch the latest news
updates and road reports. He arrived at HQ shortly before
eight to find the car park was already starting to fill up to
the point where there'd soon be no spaces left except for
those reserved for the privileged few like Willoughby and
Millership.

Monday morning started as usual with a quick round-
up of what was going on. The venue this time was one of
the small conference rooms where Moon sat on the table
swinging his legs while Thompson, Scott and Tamberlin
propped up the walls. Scott and Tamberlin began by

reporting on the results of the feelers they'd been putting out among former inmates of Winson Green Prison.

'Quite a few didn't want to talk,' said Scott who had had the splints removed from his fingers over the weekend. 'The general opinion among those that did was pretty much the same as we know already. Beames kept himself to himself most of the time. One or two mentioned about him walking round with the Bible in his hand pretending he could read it.'

'We asked them why they thought he topped himself,' said Tamberlin taking up the story. 'Most said they hadn't a clue apart from being in the nick all those years was enough to send anybody round the twist. But then we heard how upset he got when he was told his garden was going to be taken off him.'

'Garden?' Moon looked up quizzically.

'That's right,' Tamberlin continued. 'It seems going back a few years the prison authorities found a plot of land going spare at the back of one of the cell blocks and turned it over to Beames so he could grow vegetables. The staff brought in items such as bags of compost and soon he was producing all sorts of stuff which went to the prison kitchens.'

'So what happened?'

'They needed the area for something else so they had to tell Beames he couldn't grow his onions and cabbages any more. It wasn't long after when they found him hanging in his cell.'

'It's what you might call tragic,' said Scott. 'They had it in mind to find him another plot of ground but nobody got round to telling him.'

• • •

The sombre mood persisted all morning. Just before lunchtime Moon made the short trip out to the fancy dress hire shop to pick up the girls' costumes. As he came out with the costumes in a carrier bag he checked his watch. It was just coming up to twelve but, instead of driving back to HQ, he sat for a while drumming his thumbs on the steering wheel. Sheffield was only ninety minutes away, two hours at the most, but going up there in the hope of tracking down Sharon Baxter's family was frustrated by the fact that he had no idea where they lived. Then a thought struck him.

'Dave,' Thompson answered the call after three rings. 'Are you free to talk?'

'Sure Guv – what is it?'

'Cast your mind back to the press cuttings you brought back from the public library. In one of them there was an interview with Sharon Baxter's parents – have you got it to hand?'

'I will have if you give me a second.'

'There's a photograph, a bit blurry as I remember it,' Moon continued when Thompson came back on the line. 'A couple standing together in what looks like a front garden. Tell me what you see?'

'A bit of lawn, what could be some rhododendron bushes. They're standing with their backs to a road.'

'Is there a bus going by?'

'Yes, but I can't make out its number or where it's going if that's what you were hoping.'

'What's on the other side of the road?'

'I'd say at a guess it's a garden centre. There's what looks like a place for cars to park in front of a large greenhouse and a sign with a name on it.'

'Can you read it?'

'Some of the letters are hard to make out but it looks like The Potting Shed. Shall I see if I can get an address from somewhere?'

'Please.'

Moon made his next stop the car park of a supermarket where he pulled up facing a hedge of berberis and paused only to watch a goldcrest picking round among the berries. He then made his way into the self-service cafeteria where he ordered a toasted cheese sandwich. The checkouts were busy but Moon found his eyes kept drifting up towards the surveillance cameras which were everywhere and which he found unsettling even though he realised they'd been put there to catch shoplifters not detective inspectors who'd fallen out with their bosses.

When he got back to the car and checked his phone he noticed a missed call from Thompson.

'Guv, we're in luck,' Thompson said when he answered. 'There's a listing for a business called The Potting Shed in the Sheffield telephone directory. I can shout out the address and phone number if you've got a pen to hand but, if you're thinking on the lines of going up there, do you want me to get you some directions?'

'Thanks all the same, Dave. I'll find it.'

• • •

The drive to Sheffield took him through run-down pit villages where people hung about in the streets with spaced out expressions on their faces. On the outskirts of the city he stopped to top up with fuel then, a few miles further on, he pulled over to ask a postman the way to the address Thompson had given him. He came to a roundabout where he went left, away from the city, and followed a ribbon development of detached houses and bungalows dating, by the look of them, from the forties and fifties. He'd gone about a mile when he saw the garden centre on the left between a builders' merchant and a monumental mason. He pulled up far enough off the road to let the traffic behind get by then took stock of his surroundings. On the opposite side of the road was a row of bungalows and, outside one of them, an elderly man sweeping up leaves.

Getting out the car, Moon retrieved his overcoat from the back seat where it sat alongside the carrier bags containing the girls' costumes. He crossed the road in a gap in the traffic and walked the few yards to where he now had a clearer view of the man with the broom in his hands who looked to be in his late seventies. A tall stooped figure wearing a grey woolly jumper sweeping leaves into neat piles before scooping them up with his hands and putting them into a green refuse sack. He looked up and smiled when he saw Moon approaching.

'I hope you can help me,' said Moon holding up his ID. 'I'm looking for a Mr and Mrs Baxter who lived somewhere round here twenty-odd years ago.'

'I'm Jim Baxter,' said the man whose expression changed when he realised the man who'd come up and spoken to him was a police officer. 'My wife passed away some years ago, I'm afraid.'

'It's about your daughter Sharon,' Moon said. 'It may be better if we went inside.'

The man nodded and, putting the broom down next to a wheelbarrow, he led Moon up a steep flight of steps to the front door of the bungalow which was standing open. Moon glanced over his shoulder. The view from the top of the steps was the same view he remembered from the photograph. The rhododendrons had grown into a thick clump but the lawn was still there.

'I was just going to make a cup of tea,' said the man. 'Would you like one?'

'Please,' said Moon.

The man showed Moon into a small front room furnished simply yet tastefully in a style which would have been fashionable in the late fifties. He left Moon to ponder his surroundings then came back shortly afterwards carrying a tray.

'How do you take this?' he said in his soft South Yorkshire accent handing Moon a cup and saucer.

'Just a little milk, no sugar,' Moon replied realising the man was probably turning over inside with memories of what happened to his daughter. It would have been a police officer knocking on the door who brought the news which shattered the lives of him and his wife.

Moon began. 'We've received some information to suggest the man who went to prison for the murder of your daughter may have been innocent. The information may be true or it may be false but it still falls on us to investigate it as fully as we can – given the passage of time.'

The man put his tea cup down. 'I don't understand Inspector. The man they arrested confessed. What you've been told must be wrong.'

'The suggestion is the confession was extracted under duress.'

'Is he now saying he didn't kill Sharon?'

'He's dead Mr Baxter. He hung himself in his prison cell twelve months ago.'

'I'm sorry. I didn't know.'

'What it could also mean is that the person who murdered Sharon is still at large.'

The man sat with the colour slowly draining from his cheeks. 'I hoped I'd never have to relive those days. Sharon was our only child, Inspector. We had such high hopes for her. She was the first member of the family to go to university. My wife and I felt so proud when she was offered her place.'

'When did your wife pass away?'

'Fifteen years ago. She never got over Sharon's death. It broke her heart.'

'I'm sorry to be the one who has to bring back unhappy memories.'

The man shook his head. 'You've got your job to do Inspector. It can't be pleasant to have to come here today and ask questions.'

'I want to avoid this going any further than it has to,' said Moon. 'What you've gone through already is every father's worst nightmare.'

'They say time heals but it doesn't. You reach the stage where you stop thinking about it every minute of every day but the mix of anger and grief is never far away.'

'What were you told about Sharon's death?'

'That she'd been attacked with a knife. The police told us they found her by a canal.'

'You identified the body?'

'I was taken to a mortuary in Birmingham. A police car came to collect me. It was a day I'll never forget.'

'When did you learn a man had been arrested?'

'Not long afterwards. There was a phone call to say they'd pulled somebody in for questioning.'

'Did they ask you if you and your wife knew the man or if Sharon had ever mentioned his name?'

'No.'

'Didn't that strike you as odd?'

'I'm not sure I follow you.'

'I was just putting myself in the shoes of the investigating team. I would want to try to establish a motive. I'd be thinking somebody who knew Sharon would have different range of possible motives to somebody who didn't.'

'We were led to believe the murder was completely random. Sharon had the bad luck to bump into a man with a history of mental problems. It could have been anybody walking along that canal towpath. It just happened to be Sharon.'

'Where was Sharon living at the time?'

'She'd just moved into a house she was sharing with friends.'

'Was the house close to the murder scene?'

'No, it was on the same side of the city as the University. We'd helped her move in just a few weeks earlier.'

'Did it ever become apparent what Sharon was doing in the area where she was found?'

'I can't remember anybody ever bringing the subject up. We assumed she'd gone for a walk. The police thought the man must have followed her.'

'Did you know Sharon was pregnant?'

Baxter put his teacup down. 'The police told me the day I came down to identify the body. I asked them not to tell my wife. I'm not sure how she would have coped.'

'I'm sorry to have to ask you this, Mr Baxter, but did you have any idea who was the father of the child?'

'It's not a subject I find easy to talk about – I hope you understand. Did she have boyfriends? There were a few names she mentioned.'

'Did you ever meet any of them?'

'Just the one – a lad who came to the funeral.'

'Can you recall his name?'

'Yes, we kept in touch. A lad named Duncan who must be in his forties now. I still get a Christmas card from him every year.'

'Does Duncan still live in Birmingham?'

'Yes, his address is in the drawer.' Baxter rose to his feet and went across to the sideboard which was the central piece of furniture in the room.

'Here it is,' he said taking out a much thumbed address book and turning to one of the pages before handing it over to Moon.

Duncan Toogood: Moon wrote the address in his notebook including a previous address which either Baxter or his wife had crossed out at some point in the past.

'Will you be speaking to Duncan?' Baxter asked as he returned the address book to the drawer.

'I think so,' said Moon. 'Just to see if he can tell us anything useful.'

'You don't think Duncan had anything to do with Sharon's death?'

'I'll keep an open mind. I'm sure you understand.'

'He seemed such a nice lad. At the funeral we could tell he thought a lot of Sharon.'

'Did you see Duncan again? I mean after the funeral.'

'No.'

'Just the Christmas cards?'

'Yes, just the Christmas cards.'

'Apart from Duncan, did Sharon ever mention any other names?'

'There were the girls she shared the house with. One was called Marge, I can't remember the others. It's all such a long time ago.'

'Did the police ever question you about her friends?'

Baxter shook his head. 'Everything happened so quickly,' he said. 'They arrested the man and the next thing we heard was he'd confessed.'

'You took it the matter was closed? The police had got their man and that was the end of it?'

'We saw him in court. He pleaded guilty to everything.'

It was getting dark outside as Moon left. The

streetlights were starting to come on and, beyond the garden centre, the dark shape of distant hills cut a line across the sky.

'This place is getting too much for me,' said Baxter. 'Come next year I've decided to look for somewhere smaller.'

'I'll keep in touch,' said Moon.

'Please. This nightmare's gone on long enough and it's time it was brought to a close.'

• • •

Moon's journey back to Birmingham ran into early rush-hour traffic. Exhaust fumes filled the air as he crawled along behind the tail lights of a long procession of cars and trucks. An accident on the A38 caused an even bigger delay. Finally Moon pulled off the dual carriageway at a place where he knew the signal strength was good enough to make a call to Thompson.

'Dave I've got a job for you to do,' he said when the line connected then, reading from his notebook by the courtesy light, he gave Thompson the name and address of Sharon Baxter's last known boyfriend. 'Can we check out his form? I'm guessing his date of birth would have been circa 1960 – give or take a few years. See what you can come up with. I'm not expecting to find he's a serial killer but he might have some history which would give us a clue to the kind of character we're talking about.'

When he finished the call to Thompson, Moon switched off the courtesy light and sat in the dark for a while. Over to his right he could still see the line of slow moving traffic; on his left, the perimeter fence of a storage site for trailers and transport containers. He slipped on a CD of men working on railroad gangs hammering rails onto sleepers and singing as they toiled under the scorching Mississippi sun of a half a century ago. It was coming up to five according to the digital clock on the dashboard and Moon's mind went back to the stooped figure in the grey woolly jumper standing on the steps of his bungalow with memories of his dead daughter's face and a life which no longer meant anything. On the back seat of the car were the carrier bags with the girls' Hallowe'en costumes, a poignant reminder of the fragility of human happiness and how, once it's gone, it's gone forever.

CHAPTER FIVE

DUNCAN TOOGOOD

Moon didn't manage to speak to Thompson until well after ten the following morning – Thompson who, along with Tamberlin, had been busy taking statements from witnesses to an early hours stand-off between two gangs outside a takeaway where their territories met. It was business as usual on the streets of the city. The constant struggle between warring factions to control the supply of drugs and weaponry and the equally constant struggle on the part of the police to keep the lid on it.

'The address and the previous address you gave me didn't match up with anything,' Thompson reported when they sat down in Moon's office. 'A few individuals named Toogood came up who fitted the age profile but none of them had any connections with Birmingham. Do you want me to ask around to see if anybody knows him?'

'Thanks all the same, Dave, but, while we're sitting here, we could be popping round to his house to see what he has to say for himself.'

'Guv, there's something else I wanted to mention.'

'Go ahead.'

'Doing what we're doing behind Mr Willoughby's back is starting to make me feel uneasy. I know the reasons why but sooner or later we'll have to bring him in the picture so why not do it now?'

Moon looked at him. 'I understand, Dave, but it'll be my head on the chopping block if he thinks we've gone further than we should have done.'

'That's what worries me. It worries Scotty and Tambo too.'

'You want me to tell Mr Willoughby what we've unravelled so far then leave it to him to decide where it all goes next?'

'I know he could put the stoppers on everything but that's better than you ending up on a disciplinary again.'

Moon knew where Thompson was coming from. Two years before, when he was suspended, the three of them ended up being seconded to Millership and it was an experience they would find hard to forget.

'Can I think about it, Dave?'

'Sure Guv.'

• • •

Shortly after lunch Moon and Thompson headed out to the residential suburb of the city where the address he'd copied from Jim Baxter's address book was located. It was an area of red-brick terraced houses which had undergone gentrification in the last few years. What had once been the dwelling places of artisans who toiled in the local metal-bashing workshops was now home sweet home to trendy young professionals spiralling upwards towards bigger and better things.

They drew up on the side of the street which didn't have yellow lines. Moon's eye travelled along the row of newly-painted front doors until he came to the one he was looking for. He checked the time. It was just turned half past three and the daylight was already starting to go.

With a nod from Moon they got out and stood on the pavement. Thompson in his bright yellow ski jacket, Moon in his overcoat, they checked the traffic coming in both directions before crossing the road. Estate agents' signs stood outside some of the houses along with empty wheelie bins waiting for somebody to come along and put them away. They came to the house they wanted and Moon pressed the bell then waited fifteen seconds before he pressed it again.

'Looks like nobody's in,' he said staring up at the bedroom windows.

They made their way back to the car. A grey and white cat strolled lazily across the road and a woman with a child in a pushchair walked by. They sat for quarter of an hour: Moon drumming his fingers on the steering wheel; Thompson passing the time fiddling with the clock settings on his phone.

'He could be at work,' said Thompson when he finished.

'Let's give it a few more minutes,' said Moon noticing the shadows getting longer and a few of the cars coming up the road with their lights on.

It was Thompson who spotted the man walking towards them wearing a ski jacket not unlike his own. He carried a rucksack over one shoulder and a plastic carrier bag in his hand. When he drew closer Moon saw he was about six feet tall, clean shaven with dark brown hair cut short and combed back off his face. He stopped in front of the door where Moon and Thompson had tried ringing the bell earlier and took a bunch of keys out of his pocket.

'Quick,' said Moon and, in a flash, he and Thompson were out of the car and dashing across the road again.

'Mr Toogood?' said Moon as he came up behind holding his ID in his hand. The man turned round. 'I'm Detective Inspector Moon. This is Detective Sergeant Thompson. We'd like a word with you please. Inside, if you don't mind.'

The man looked startled. 'You're police?'

'Serious crimes officers,' said Moon taking in the man's increasingly alarmed look.

The front door opened onto a hallway with a staircase going off and a row of pegs along the wall. Moon noticed a cycling helmet hanging off one of the pegs.

'You must excuse the mess,' said the man leading them through into a room with windows back and front looking like a dividing wall had been knocked through at some point. The room was lined with bookshelves while a Persian rug took away the bareness of the varnished oak floorboards. There was a gas fire in a tiled Victorian surround which looked like the original.

'Please sit down,' said the man clearing a space on the sofa which was littered with papers. 'You will have gathered I don't have many visitors.'

'You're Mr Duncan Toogood?' said Moon watching the man as he bent over to light the fire.

'I can't think what this is about,' he replied. 'Is it to do with something that's happened at school?'

'I understand you knew a young woman named Sharon Baxter who was found dead in 1978.'

'Sharon? Yes I did. We were at university together.'

'You went out with her? Boyfriend and girlfriend so to speak?'

'For a few months. I met her at the Freshers' Ball and it went from there.'

'You were going out with her at the time of her death?'

'No, she'd finished with me long before then.'

Moon and Thompson exchanged glances.

'Can you be more precise about the dates?' Moon said.

'The Freshers' Ball would have been at the start of term in September and I'd say it was just before the Easter vac when she called it off.'

'So we're talking about March or April depending on when Easter fell in 1978?'

'Yes.'

'What happened?'

'The usual story, I suppose. She met somebody else.'

'Another student?'

'No, he was older than Sharon. Not a pleasant character but, for some reason, she saw something in him.'

'Any clue to what the attraction could have been?'

'He drove round in a sports car at a time when most of us caught the bus if it was too far to go on our bikes.'

'Did you go on seeing Sharon after she broke off with you?'

'We were in the same faculty and shared the same friends so we could hardly avoid bumping into one another.'

'I meant did you go out on dates?'

'I did try to win her back at the start of summer term but she cold-shouldered me and in the end I gave up. In the back of my mind was one day she might come to her senses.'

'I take it she didn't?'

Toogood didn't answer. He stood staring into the flames of the fire, tormented perhaps by the stirring of old memories.

Moon continued. 'Did you know she was pregnant?'

'It wasn't me if that's what you're thinking.'

'You seem very sure.'

Toogood turned round so he was facing Moon, the light from the fire ruddying his cheeks. 'The relationship between Sharon and I never went as far as having sex and, before I answer any more of your questions, can you tell me what this is about?'

Moon looked at him. 'The man who went to prison for Sharon's murder may have been wrongly convicted. He confessed but, from what we've been told, the confession should never have been allowed to stand.'

'You mean somebody else killed Sharon?'

'We're not saying anything until we know more.'

'You don't think I did it?'

Moon's face remained a blank. 'Like I said Mr Toogood we'll reserve judgment until we have more information.'

'I loved Sharon. What possible motive could I have had for wanting to kill her?'

'She jilted you.'

'Yes but I would never have hurt her.'

'You asked me for a possible motive and I gave you one.'

'All the same...'

'Perhaps we should continue,' said Moon after a long pause in which the silence was only interrupted by the hissing of the gas fire and the sound of a car alarm going off somewhere outside in the street. 'Going back to the murder, how did you first get to hear about it?'

'There was a headline on the front page of the evening paper saying the body of a girl had been found by a canal. It didn't name her but one of her housemates told me the police had been round asking questions.'

'Did the police question you?'

'No.'

'Didn't that strike you as odd seeing the two of you had been an item up to a few months before?'

'I thought nothing of it at the time. It was only a matter of days before they arrested a man and he confessed.'

'Did you know the man?'

'No, I'd never heard of him before. He lived somewhere near to where Sharon's body was found.'

'Was it a district Sharon knew?' This came from Thompson. Thompson was sitting on the arm of a chair near the door.

'She'd only been living in Birmingham since September.'

'What about you?'

'It's not somewhere I've ever visited.'

'What do you think she was doing there?'

'I have no idea.'

'You must have given it some thought.'

'I assumed it was where the man they arrested took her.'

'Where were you living at the time this happened?'

'On campus in one of the student halls of residence.'

Moon took over the questioning again. 'Can we go back to the man Sharon started going out with when she finished with you? You described him as not a very pleasant character. Was there any reason you formed this view?'

'He didn't treat Sharon nicely. Yes, I know it sounds like sour grapes, but he seemed to have some kind of hold over her which nobody could understand. There were rumours he knocked her about but I couldn't say whether they were true or not.'

'You were all students. What brought him into your circle?'

'He hung around in one of the pubs we used to use. He tried to latch onto the girls.'

'Including Sharon?'

'Including Sharon.'

'You make him sound like a Lothario.'

'Looking back, it would be a fair way to describe him. Some people said he was two-timing Sharon but, again, I couldn't say whether it was true or not.'

'Was he still going out with Sharon at the time of her death?'

'I believe so but I can't be absolutely sure. I tried my best to stay out of the mess she seemed to be making of her life.'

'Can you recall his name?'

'Jake Morris. It's not a name I could easily forget.'

'Did the police interview him in connection with the murder?'

'That I don't know. As you can imagine, we were scarcely on speaking terms.'

'What happened to him?'

'After Sharon's death I never saw him again. I went to her funeral in Sheffield and half-expected to see him there but he didn't show.'

'What did you think?'

'It was proof to me he had no real feelings for her.'

'How did you find out Sharon was pregnant?'

'It filtered its way back to me several months afterwards.'

'Did you think Morris was responsible?'

'For getting her pregnant? I don't know Inspector. It's not a subject I care to dwell on.'

'Apart from his name, can you recall anything else about Morris? Where he lived, for example, or where he worked?'

'He was the kind who never gave away much about himself. Shifty, when I think back.'

'And you say he was older than you and your friends?'

'I'd guess he was about twenty-five at the time we knew him.'

'Are you still in touch with any of the people you knew at university?'

'A few of them.'

'Has anybody ever mentioned Morris in recent years?'

'Funnily enough his name came up in a conversation not long ago.'

'How come?'

'We had a get-together organised by an alumni group I belong to. We met up at a tapas bar in town and there were a lot of old faces there, faces I hadn't seen for years. I got talking to somebody who asked me out of the blue if I'd seen Morris recently.'

'You said you hadn't?'

'Exactly.'

'Where did the conversation go from there?'

'Nowhere really. The woman who asked me about Morris didn't explain why she was interested.'

'Was this woman one of Sharon's friends?'

'Loosely. She wasn't one of the girls Sharon shared the house with but she was part of the crowd.'

'Was that it?'

'More or less.'

'What's this woman's name?'

'Trish. Trish Phillips. She does counselling for a living. She lives somewhere out in the country.'

''Did she have a view of Morris?'

'She didn't like him. She'd heard about somebody who'd had a relationship with him and she tried to warn Sharon off.'

'Do you have an address or phone number for her?'

'I've got her phone number – she gave it to me as I left the tapas bar. There were all the normal promises about keeping in touch.'

'Have you spoken to her since?

'I keep saying I'll ring her and arrange to meet up for a drink but I haven't got round to it.'

'You don't go out much?'

Toogood smiled. 'I suppose you could say I'm a bit of a recluse.'

'What do you do for a living?'

'I teach at the local comprehensive school. I'm Head of English.'

'You live alone?'

'I never married, Inspector. Sharon was the love of my life. There could never be anybody after her.'

'Twenty-three years is a long time for grieving.'

'So everybody keeps telling me.'

CHAPTER SIX

THE COUNSELLOR

IT WAS MID-AFTERNOON WHEN MOON MADE THE turn off the main road which took him down a winding country lane with steep banks on either side. The shadows were already starting to spread out as the sun sank lower in the sky. Almost a week had gone by since he and Thompson had paid their visit to Duncan Toogood; a week in which Moon had busied himself with paperwork and thinking through his next move.

The lane came to an end next to a field gateway where two cars and a tractor were parked on the stubble. Moon saw at once the narrow track in front flanked by beds of nettles and overhanging hedges. Unfastening his seat belt he got out of the car and stretched his legs while taking in the view. A fresh breeze stirred in the air bringing with it the distant sound of sheep and the high piercing cry of a buzzard coming from somewhere high up in the sky where he couldn't see it. He reached in the back seat for his overcoat and, after putting it on, he set off down the narrow track following the directions he'd been given. He noticed at once the musty smells: the scent of a fox perhaps or the rotting smell of dead leaves composting beneath the hedgerows. Soon he heard the sound of the river up in front then, twenty yards further on, he got his first glimpse of it through the trees. Brown turgid waters swollen by recent rain twisting around a fallen elm making whorls and whirlpools.

He took a path to the left along the river bank which brought him to a rickety plank bridge across a tumbling brook where a handrail had been provided for people to steady themselves. The planks were slippery, coated with slime and moss, and Moon was already starting to regret not changing out of his smooth-soled city shoes into the pair of wellingtons he kept in the boot of the car. Beyond the bridge, the path carried on but on his left was the white gate he'd been told to look out for. Once through the gate he found himself in what at first appeared to be a tangled wilderness until he realised he was looking at a carefully tended garden of herbs and wild plants. The garden rose up in terraces to the top of a bank where a cottage with lime-washed walls and a roof of Welsh slates stood.

'This way,' called a voice and Moon looked up to see the figure of a woman in jeans and a tweed jacket standing at the door of the cottage pointing to a flight of steps. He raised his hand to acknowledge he'd heard her over the noise of the brook coming from behind. The steps were steep and he found the effort of climbing them made him out of puff.

'Welcome to the country,' said the woman smiling and holding out a hand to shake. 'Trish Phillips, in case you hadn't guessed. Your call yesterday didn't come as a surprise. Duncan rang after you'd been to see him. I think he was worried about giving you my number without speaking to me first.'

'It was good of you to find time to see me,' said Moon taking in details of her appearance: rosy cheeks with a fresh outdoor complexion; hair cut short in a simple no-nonsense bob, blue eyes and no make-up.

'I only work three days a week,' she said. 'I had no plans for today so it fitted in nicely.'

Moon wiped his feet on a coconut mat placed just inside the door of the cottage before following her along a passageway of unevenly laid quarry tiles into an old-fashioned country kitchen. A wood-fired cast-iron stove gave out heat and, in front of it, a basket where a large tabby cat lay curled up fast asleep. She took his overcoat from him and hung it on a peg at the back of the door.

'I don't do tea in the afternoon,' she said as she switched on a coffee machine which was standing ready. 'I gather you want to talk about Sharon Baxter. Duncan explained what it was about. Poor Duncan, he never got over her.' She perched on a stool and indicated to Moon to do the same.

'You knew Sharon?' he asked.

'We had an on and off relationship. Sometimes we were pally, other times we weren't.'

'What about at the time of her death?'

'We hadn't spoken to one another for months.'

'Was there a reason?'

'I think Duncan has told you about Jake Morris. I discovered she was going out with him and I told her what I thought.'

'Which was what?'

'She was stupid to dump Duncan for somebody like him.'

'She didn't like it?'

'She told me it was none of my business.'

'What had you got against Morris?'

'A long list of things.'

'Yet Sharon had a crush on him?'

'Like a silly little school-girl when I think back.'

'Duncan said there were rumours he knocked her about.'

'I heard the same stories.'

'Did it surprise you?'

'I can't say it did. He always struck me as a bully – the sort who wouldn't think twice about using his fists.'

'Did you know Sharon was pregnant?'

'She didn't tell me herself. By then we were no longer on speaking terms.'

'What did you think?'

'Everybody knew she was sleeping with Morris.'

'Did you consider she could have been seeing someone else apart from him? Another boyfriend nobody knew about?'

'If she was she kept it very quiet. Not easy to do in a houseful of students.'

'You knew the girls she lived with?'

'They were the first to learn about her body being found. The police came to the house one afternoon after lectures.'

'What happened next?'

'We heard somebody had been arrested.'

'What about Morris?'

'We never saw him again. Not that anybody missed him.'

'When you left university did you keep in touch with your friends?'

'For a time, yes, then I took up a teaching post in Spain and, when I came back five years later, I found most of them had moved on.'

'You went to a reunion party recently which is where you bumped into Duncan.'

'These invitations come in the post from time to time. Deciding to go was a last minute thing.'

'Why did you ask Duncan if he'd seen Morris?'

'I do counselling – Duncan may have told you. People referred to me by their GPs or people who come to me because they've been given my name by somebody they know – anxiety and depression cases mostly. One day a woman I'll refer to as Sarah rang up to make an appointment.'

'This woman was suffering from depression?'

'She'd been unwell for a long time, all sorts of strange symptoms, but there was no obvious physical cause. She'd been prescribed anti-depressants but she'd stopped taking them. She was single, in her forties, living in a nice apartment with lots of friends yet something had completely thrown her.'

'Did you ever get to the root of it?'

'I can't say I did. Something had happened to her a long time ago. Something she'd bottled up. Something she couldn't bring herself to talk about – but what you want to know is what any of this has got to do with Jake Morris and why I asked Duncan if he'd seen him. The answer is to do with Sarah – which was the reason why I mentioned her.'

The coffee finished filtering and Trish broke off to pour two mugs. The cat stretched in its basket then went back to sleep again.

'I can't remember how it first came up,' Trish continued after she brought the coffee across. 'Sarah told me she had a sister and, during the course of one of our sessions she just happened to mention that she – the sister that is – had been drawn into a relationship with somebody Sarah hated.'

'You're not going to tell me the relationship was with Morris?'

'Yes, I know it's an amazing coincidence but paths do cross in life and sometimes they're meant to. Sarah said a number of things which gave me a clue. In the end I asked her.'

'What else did she tell you?'

'It seemed Sarah saw from the start Morris was a bad lot and she tried to get her sister to see she was making a mistake.'

'What did her sister have to say?'

'She told Sarah to stop interfering. Listening to Sarah was like having the conversations I'd had with Sharon Baxter played back to me.'

'The sister stuck up for Morris?'

'Just like Sharon, she made excuses for him. When he stood her up, she pretended it hadn't happened. When he was rude to their friends, she tried to pass it off as a joke.'

'Are you saying the cause of Sarah's breakdown was linked to what she saw happening to her sister?'

'Something had affected her but she never told me what it was.'

'Where's Sarah now?'

'In a better place than she was. You could say she's still work in progress. She comes to see me from time to time when – in her words – she starts to feel wobbly.'

'You've not said what became of the sister.'

'Sarah hasn't spoken to her for years. For some reason the two of them chose to go their separate ways but something else Sarah told me was that her sister and Morris tied the knot some time back in the eighties. Soon after they got married they bought a house somewhere out in stockbroker country.'

'They don't sound short of money.'

'According to Sarah, Morris runs his own business – something to do with personal injury claims.'

'Did Duncan tell you about the man who went to prison for Sharon's murder?'

'I gather he may have been innocent.'

'He hung himself in his prison cell at the end of last year. By then he'd done over twenty years of a life sentence.'

'I take it this is why you're asking questions about Morris? Is there a theory he could have been the one who killed Sharon? He knifed her because he wanted to get rid of the child she was carrying?'

'What do you think?'

Trish topped up the coffee. 'From what I saw I wouldn't put anything past him. Sharon the cute little dolly-bird sitting next to him in his sports car was one thing. Sharon pushing a pram and coming after him for money would not have gone down well with him. Did Duncan tell you about Liz Woodall?'

'Liz who?'

'A girl Morris went out with before any of us knew him.'

'What about her?'

'She met a sticky end. A drowning accident somewhere down on the South Coast.'

'How do you know this?'

'There was a barmaid who worked in the pub we used. She told us.'

'You say a drowning accident?'

'Her body was found on a beach. She'd not been seen in Birmingham for weeks.'

'What about the barmaid?'

'I only knew her as Bridget. The pub isn't there anymore.'

'Was Bridget suggesting Morris may have had something to do with this girl's death?'

'She was just passing on what she'd heard.'

'Which was what?'

'Liz left town to get away from him. Apparently he'd been threatening what he was going to do to her. He'd already beaten her up a few times.'

'Did any of this come out in the wake of Sharon's death?'

'Bridget wouldn't go to the police. She was scared Morris would find out. She didn't want to be the next dead girl.'

CHAPTER SEVEN

SID MARPLES

MOON WAS SO DEEPLY LOST IN HIS THOUGHTS HE nearly jumped out of his skin when the phone rang. It was ten past ten – the day after he'd been to see Trish Phillips and he was sitting alone in his office staring at the dregs in the bottom of his empty coffee cup.

'Charlie.' It was Lionel Moet sounding bright and chipper for a cold wet November morning. 'Charlie, I finally found my old diaries in the bottom of a drawer where I'd forgotten I'd put them. The officer who led the investigation into the girl from Yorkshire's murder was Detective Chief Inspector Marples – a brusque fellow as I remember him. I believe he went on to bigger and better things but the memory fails, alas.'

'Sid Marples?'

'I can't think we were ever on first name terms – there again, things were more formal in those days. Did you know him?'

'Before my time, Nell, but I've heard him mentioned a few times.'

'I imagine he must be retired. He may have croaked it for all I know.'

Quarter of an hour later Thompson, Scott and Tamberlin trooped in for the meeting Moon had called to bring them up to speed on what he'd learned from speaking to Trish Phillips.

'The information about the girl washed up on the beach is hearsay and may not be reliable,' Moon added when he'd finished. 'It's important therefore we keep an open mind. Morris doesn't sound like the kind of character any of us would want to invite round for Sunday lunch but it doesn't make him a murderer. In summary, we still have a long way to go to prove whether Wilson Beames was innocent or not. We may never get there.'

'Guv.' This came from Thompson. 'Apart from somewhere on the South Coast, you've not said yet where this girl's body was found.'

'According to Trish Phillips, somewhere near Lyme Regis – I gather we're talking about 1971 or '72. It may be the girl fell in the sea and drowned or there may be more to it. One way or another we need to find out.'

'1971 was thirty years ago,' said Tamberlin. 'We're going to be hard pushed to find many people who go back that far.'

Moon fixed a look on him. 'This is where two smart young detectives like Scotty and you have a chance to come into your own. Consider it part of your personal development. One day you'll thank me for all the time and effort I've put into making the pair of you useful.'

'Do we get to go to the seaside?' said Scott with a cheeky grin on his face.

'Not if it involves making expenses claims for sticks of rock and rides on donkeys,' Moon replied. He turned back to Thompson. 'Dave, see what you can do to put a bit more flesh on what we know about this character Morris. See if he's got any form – and see if you can put your finger on anything which would give us a clue to why the police back in the seventies would want to protect him. Also we've now got the identity of the senior officer who was responsible for Beames' arrest but, before we start treading on too many toes, I'll see what I can learn about him through unofficial channels first.'

• • •

It was just after two when Moon pulled up on a piece of spare land next to the entrance to a building site. It had been raining all day and the roadways onto the site were already turning into a sea of grey mud. He wondered about changing into his wellingtons but then he saw somebody had thoughtfully laid a path of duckboards to the portacabin positioned just inside the chain link fence which ran round the perimeter of the construction work. As he turned his coat collar up against the rain his eyes fell on the guard dog warning notices attached to the fence and another warning to say CCTV cameras were in operation. A flat bed truck laden with scaffolding poles had just arrived and a team of men in hard hats and high vis jackets were standing ready to unload it. The door of the portacabin opened outwards and Moon immediately noticed the smell of stale cigarettes wafting from inside.

'I didn't expect to hear from you quite so soon,' said Alf Stepney rising to his feet to shake hands. 'On the phone it sounded like you had something private you wanted to talk about. Cup of tea suit you? I'm afraid we don't stretch to much round here.'

Stepney went over to a table in the corner where he switched on a kettle and waited for it to come to the boil. Moon meanwhile took in details of the portacabin's sparse interior. A desk and a collection of chairs which looked like they'd been thrown out of an office years ago. A CCTV monitor with grey flickering images on the screen. An ashtray on the desk filled to overflowing.

'I'm guessing something's come up,' said Stepney bringing two mugs across. 'You've not come out here in the pissing rain just to talk over old times.'

'Sid Marples,' said Moon taking one of the mugs off him. 'He must have been around in your time.'

'What about him?'

'I want to know what made him tick.'

'You're forgetting something, Charlie. The agreement I signed. My lips are sealed when it comes to talking about things which went on years ago. One careless slip of the tongue on my part and they could be coming after me to claw back the money they paid me – the money I haven't got any more.'

'Sid Marples led the investigation into a murder back in 1978. A student named Sharon Baxter who was stabbed to death. It was in all the papers.'

'I was still in Swansea in 1978. I didn't come to Birmingham until 1981.'

'Was Sid Marples still around?'

'He was Detective Superintendent Marples when I knew him. Later on he took up a position at the Home Office. He retired with a gong at about the time they gave me the push. He died soon after; cerebral haemorrhage, so I heard.'

'A man with the mind of a ten year old went to prison for something he didn't do – a man who ended up hanging himself.'

Stepney stared into his cup. Moon noticed his uniform was frayed at the cuffs and the nicotine stains on his fingers.

'What do you want from me, Charlie?' he said after the silence had gone on for a while.

'I'm working on the theory Marples was protecting somebody.'

'What if I say I can't help?'

'I'd walk away from here today thinking I'd got you wrong. I thought you stood for what was right and proper but you turned out to be as bad as the rest.'

Stepney smiled. 'You've always been your own man, Charlie. I respect you for it. I know what it feels like standing in your shoes and wondering whether it's worth the hassle of having pricks like Willoughby on your back all the time. Sid Marples was a paedo. It went back to when he was a constable on the beat and he caught Little Johnny nicking sweets out of the sweet shop. He told Little Johnny he wouldn't run him in providing he went in the public toilets and did what he was told to do. We're back in the fifties, Charlie, when kids like Little Johnny stood to attention when they were spoken to by a policeman. If they said anything to their mums and dads they'd probably end up with a smack round the head for telling lies. As Sid rose through the ranks his techniques for procuring young lads became more subtle. Who would he want to protect? I'd say himself comes top of the list.'

'How much of this was common knowledge?'

'Why didn't anybody report him? This was where he was clever. He made it his business to find out who was taking backhanders, who was having it off with the station sergeant's wife, who was getting a cut from the dealer on the street corner. Don't tell on me and I won't tell on you was the motto he lived by. You have to say it worked for him. Everybody was shit-scared of Sid Marples. You cross him and you paid for it. You go along with him and you kept out of trouble. He surrounded himself with a mob of heavies – bent coppers who enjoyed his patronage and acted as his enforcers.'

'What about you?'

'I did my best to steer clear of him. I consoled myself with the thought he'd get his come-uppance one day but there I was wrong. He climbed even higher up the ladder to the point where he became untouchable.'

'Where does Willoughby fit in?'

'He doesn't. He came after Sid went off to grace the corridors of Whitehall. Sid was long gone when the shit hit the fan in 1989. What Willoughby knows about Sid and what he doesn't would be speculation on my part.'

'Did you hear anything else?'

'There was a rumour doing the rounds about a ring of paedos operating in the police up to and around the time Sid disappeared from the local scene. If it was true, then he would have been one of the leading lights. Like I said, he became more subtle as the years went by. All I ever heard were whispers.'

It was still raining when Moon stepped back outside.

'Remember you didn't hear any of this from me,' said Stepney as he stood at the door of the portacabin to see him off. 'Remember too raking up what went on years ago can be a dangerous game. Take it from me. I'm somebody who knows.'

'You think I should just shrug my shoulders and walk off?'

Stepney smiled. 'We must meet up for that drink some time, Charlie. Leaving these things too long can be a mistake.'

• • •

The streetlights were coming on and a rocket went up in the sky as Moon drove back into the city reminding him it was just a few days to go to Guy Fawkes Night. Using the hands-free he gave Jo a ring in the hope of catching her and, when she answered, he arranged to meet up in the coffee shop of a department store in the centre of the city.

They arrived at almost exactly the same time. Moon spotted Jo in front of him on the escalator and together they went to the self-service counter of the coffee shop where they ordered two Americanos. Trade was slack on a cold wet November afternoon in the middle of the week and they sat at a table well out of earshot of the handful of shoppers who were the only other customers.

'I know Trish Phillips,' Jo said when Moon had finished filling her in. 'She's done a lot of work with victims of domestic violence and I've spoken to her a few times to do with the series of articles I'm writing. So tell me, Charlie, where do we go from here?'

'We're seeing what we can find out about the girl who was washed up on the beach. It might lead us onto something. There again, it might not.'

'In short, all this could still come to nothing?'

'There's something else,' Moon said then he told her what he'd just learned from Alf Stepney.

Jo sat in silence for a few minutes. In the background the clatter of cups and saucers and the noise of roadworks coming from the street outside.

'I'll keep this information about Marples to myself for the time being,' Moon added. 'I'll use it if I have to but I'd rather see what else turns up first.'

'How do you know this man Stepney's telling you the truth?'

'Did he make it up? Has he got some grudge against Sid Marples I don't know about? Is he trying to set me up? I haven't a clue, Jo. I'm just hoping something will turn up soon to tell me.'

CHAPTER EIGHT

THE TOOL REPAIRER

GUY FAWKES NIGHT FELL ON A MONDAY AND MOON kept to the promise he'd made to the girls to take them to the park to watch the fireworks. Standing in the dark with the smell of bonfire smoke and baked potatoes wafting round took him back to his own childhood and memories of his father – a man of few words for whom family life seemed to be something he struggled with. A figure who came through the door at half past five every night yet stood back from being drawn in too close. Like father, like son, Moon wondered as the girls, sparklers in hands, jumped up and down with the excitement of each flash and bang. But never far from his thoughts in recent days was the image of Sharon Baxter's father, an elderly man who swept up leaves in the garden of a bungalow which had become too big for him. A man for whom past memories came with an unbearably bitter taste.

• • •

The first sight to greet Moon when he arrived at the office two days later was that of Millership standing by the side of his car examining a chip in the paintwork.

'Morning Charlie,' Millership said when he noticed Moon walking by.

'Morning,' said Moon not stopping to engage in further conversation. Instead he kept walking, taking a short cut into the building through a fire door somebody had left open.

Thompson was attending a mediation meeting at his solicitor's office connected with his impending divorce so the morning get-together was just Moon, Scott and Tamberlin sitting round Moon's desk and Moon listening to what the other two had to say.

'The information you received was correct,' Scott began. 'The girl's body was found washed up on a beach near Lyme Regis in September 1971 looking like it had been in the water for a few days. They identified her from her fingerprints – it seems she'd been done for possession of drugs a few times. Elizabeth Anne Woodall. Date of birth: 19.04.1952, making her nineteen at the time of her death. Last known address: sheltered accommodation in Worcester where she'd been living for three months.'

'We had to ask around to find anybody who went back as far as the seventies,' said Tamberlin taking up the story. 'Finally we got put on to a retired detective constable who'd been involved in the case. It was from him we learned the body was fully clothed when it was washed up ruling out the possibility of it belonging to somebody who'd got into difficulties swimming. We were told the currents are notoriously treacherous off that stretch of coast so the conclusion everybody came to, including the coroner, was she'd got too close to the water just as a big wave came in. She had no connections locally as far as anybody knew and nobody had reported her missing. What she was doing down on the South Coast was a mystery but there was speculation she may have been sleeping rough.'

'You mentioned she'd been living in sheltered accommodation,' said Moon. 'What was that about?'

'We haven't a clue,' Tamberlin replied. 'The name of the place where she'd been staying was Cobb House which stuck in everybody's memory because The Cobb is a famous landmark in Lyme Regis. We tried running it through the system but nothing came up so we're assuming it's no longer there.'

• • •

Moon left it until after lunch before he rang Jo.

'I'm guessing a refuge for women in a provincial city like Worcester would have been pretty unique thirty years ago,' she said when Moon finished explaining why he was trying to pick her brains. 'Some of these places were run by charities, others had public funding. Often, though, they didn't last very long thanks to local residents getting up in arms because they thought men with histories of violence would be drawn to the areas where they were located. Pimps coming after girls who were trying to get off the game. Drug pushers looking for anybody who might be vulnerable. Letters to the Council to do something about it, petitions: you name it. Do you want me to ask around Charlie?'

'Please.'

'I'll keep your name out of it. Pretend it's me doing research for one of my articles.'

• • •

It was later in the afternoon when Thompson put his head round the door. Thompson had a glum look on his face thanks, Moon guessed, to a miserable morning spent arguing the toss with his soon to be ex-wife and her solicitor about how big a slice of his salary it would take to keep her in the manner to which she'd become accustomed.

'The job you asked me to do,' Thompson said as he stood as he often did with one arm resting on top of of the filing cabinet. 'I tried running a criminal records check on men with local connections named Jake or Jacob Morris born late forties or early fifties and drew a complete blank. It occurred to me too Jake could be an alias or a nickname so, without more detail, I started to feel I was achieving nothing apart from pissing in the wind. Then I remembered the information about Morris being involved in a business to do with accident claims and, on the off-chance, I asked my solicitor this morning if the name meant anything to her.'

'What did she say?'

'She referred me to one of her colleagues who just happened to be free. He acts on behalf of a number of leading public liability and legal expenses insurers so he knows what's what when it comes to claims artists and ambulance chasers.'

'He'd heard of Morris?'

'He told me off the record Morris trades under the name of JCM Litigation and has the reputation of being a bit of a shyster.'

'Do you know where he operates from?'

'I've written down the address of his registered office,' Thompson replied handing Moon a sheet of paper. 'I then checked with Companies' House and found out his full name is Jacob Crichton Morris which I ran through criminal records again but, again, nothing showed up. It could mean he's clean or it could mean what we think – he had pals in the right places who were there at the right time to cover up for him. I've also got a home address where, according to the Electoral Register, he and his wife have been living since 1982.'

'What else do we know?'

'Not a lot. I did a bit of asking round and found out he's a member of the golf club near to where he lives and takes a keen interest in restoring classic sports cars. His wife involves herself in the local Women's Institute – makes cakes for the Church bring-and-buy sale, that sort of thing. They don't appear to have any kids.'

'Any gossip?'

'He doesn't go down well with the crowd at the golf club. He tries to act the part of the country gent but he can't cut it, if you know what I mean. She's got the reputation for being cold and stand-offish. I can keep asking round but it's up to you how much further you want me to go.'

'Leave it there for now, Dave. I don't want word getting back to him we've been asking questions. Anything else?'

Thompson shuffled his feet. 'Only to say I've heard this Sid Marples who led the investigation into the girl's murder was a big player in his day.'

'What of it?'

'We're building a case for taking him down. You, me, Scotty and Tambo versus the rest.'

'You're saying we should drop what we're doing?'

'You know what I'm saying, Guv. We could be getting in over our heads.'

Moon looked at him. Keeping Alf Stepney's name out of it meant Thompson knew nothing about the paedophile allegations.

'Trust me, Dave. I know what I'm doing.'

Thompson nodded. 'I'm sorry Guv. I had to say what was going through my mind.'

• • •

Two days later Jo rang to say she had some news and they arranged to meet for a sandwich at a pub in town they both knew. It was just after midday when Moon left site. It was the start of the second week of November and, as he drove through the city streets looking for somewhere to park, he noticed the shop windows filled with tacky reminders Christmas wasn't far away.

Jo was sitting in a corner with a glass of wine when he arrived and, after stopping off at the bar to pick up a drink for himself, he went over to join her. They ordered food first then Jo took the reporter's notebook out of the bag she always carried when she was working and flicked through the pages.

'Cobb House in Worcester closed in 1979,' she began. 'I found this out from one of the collaborators I've been working with who goes back to the early days of bringing the issue of domestic violence into the public eye. She gave me the name of Alice Cobb who is the woman who started the place and, at one time, ran it almost single-handed. I found out Alice still lives in a village on the edge of the Wyre Forest where I made contact with her. Luckily for me, she'd read some of my articles so there was no need for lengthy introductions. She's well into her eighties but her recollection of time and events was remarkable for somebody of her age. Liz Woodall stayed at Cobb House in the summer of 1971 shortly before her death. Alice confirmed she originally came from Birmingham but, guess what, she moved to Worcester to get away from a boyfriend who'd beaten her up a few times. Liz and another sibling had spent a lot of time in children's homes and, according to Alice, it was a sad story: mother and father split up; mother on drugs; children neglected and taken into care.'

'Do we know why she decided to leave Cobb House?'

'The boyfriend got wind of where she was staying. She was terrified of what he would come and do to her.'

'Was the boyfriend Morris?'

'According to Alice Liz never mentioned his name but she did tell me something else interesting. Earlier this year she had a letter forwarded to her which was from Liz's younger brother, Andrew. He'd been trying for a while to find out more about what happened to Liz in the last few weeks of her life. He'd put his phone number in the letter and Alice rang him but only to say she couldn't be much help. When I said I'd like to speak to Andrew, Alice agreed to see if he had any objections to her giving me his number. When I got home last night there was a message on the machine to ring Alice which I did. It appears Andrew is happy to talk so it's left to me to phone him. He still lives in Birmingham.'

The sandwiches arrived and Moon asked the girl who brought them for two more glasses of wine.

'How do you want me to play this?' Jo said. 'I'm not comfortable about fixing up to meet Liz's brother then turning up with you in tow. Trying to pass you off as another journalist would be ridiculous because people like me don't go round in pairs.'

'You'd rather be up front?'

'What do you think?'

'I think you're right. There's no point in getting off on the wrong foot. He could be our best bet for building a case against Morris. On the other hand, if he knows nothing or he's not prepared to talk it's best we know.'

• • •

It was two o'clock the following afternoon when Moon took the call from Jo.

'I've spoken to Andrew Woodall,' she said with her voice breaking up because of the poor signal in Moon's office. 'I think he was surprised to learn the police are still interested in the death of his sister after all this time but he's happy to help in whatever way he can because he's convinced the truth never came out about what really happened to her. He told me he works nights but he could meet us any evening before his shift starts.'

'Did he say where?'

'He gave me the name of a pub.'

'How did you leave it?'

'I said I'd get back to him.'

• • •

Moon picked Jo up outside her apartment. It was just before six which left plenty of time to make the short journey across town in the rush hour traffic to the place where she'd arranged to meet the brother of the girl who was found washed up on a beach thirty years before. There were a few spots of rain on the windscreen as they passed through the busy streets. Moon flicked the wipers occasionally while Jo sat in silence with her eyes fixed on the tail lights of traffic in front.

'This looks like it,' she said pointing to a poorly lit pub sign in the rundown part of the city they were passing through. Moon pulled up outside where they sat and waited. It was twenty past six and they were ten minutes early. The rain was now coming down steadily. On the other side of the road there was a parade of shops where a takeaway was doing a brisk trade. A few cars went by but none of them stopped. Finally they decided it was time to make a move and, with Moon in his overcoat and Jo sheltering under her umbrella, they walked the few yards to the front door of the pub where there was a light on over the porch. Once inside, they followed the sound of voices which led them into a bar where three men stood drinking who looked up when they walked in. There was a big screen television on the wall tuned to a sports channel but, apart from the three men, the place was empty.

'Roy, you've got customers,' one of the men shouted to somebody who was invisible before turning back to Moon and grinning. Presently a man in shirtsleeves appeared and Moon asked for a glass of white wine for Jo while choosing a pint of bitter for himself sensing a man who drank wine might look out of place in these surroundings. The three men went back to watching the television while Moon joined Jo over in the corner where she'd taken a seat.

On the dot of half past six, a tall stooping figure in a rain-soaked donkey jacket walked in and, spotting Jo and Moon, he came and spoke to them.

'I'm Andy,' he said. The three men at the bar looked across briefly before turning their attention back to the television where highlights of a football match were being shown.

Andy shook his head when Moon offered to buy him a beer and asked for lemonade instead.

'Our shift manager is red hot on people reporting for work with the smell of alcohol on their breath,' he explained.

Moon nodded. He put Andy as somebody in his early to mid forties – softly spoken with a receding hairline and the ghostly pallor of a man who works nights. When Moon brought the glass of lemonade across he sat sipping it slowly waiting for one of them to speak.

'Thank you for agreeing to meet us,' Moon began. 'The questions I've got concern your sister Elizabeth and what happened to her. I appreciate we're going back a long way and I'm guessing you would have only been a child at the time.'

'I didn't know about Liz's death until weeks afterwards. A woman from Social Services came to see me. She told me to be brave. I can remember thinking it was a funny thing to say to somebody who'd spent his whole life having to be brave.'

'Where were you living at the time?'

'At the children's home where I'd been put the year before.'

'Did you see much of your sister?'

'She was older. Sometimes she came to visit but not often.'

'Can you recall the last time you saw her?'

'She brought me a birthday card. She said she was sorry for it being late. It would have been about six months before I heard about her body being found.'

'How did she seem?'

Andy shrugged. 'She didn't say a lot but, there again, she was never one for talking.'

'Did you know what was going on in her life at the time of her death?'

Andy shook his head. 'We were never that close. I was her eleven year old brother – a kid. She never shared her secrets with me.'

'Did you look forward to her visits?' This came from Jo who'd been studying Andy's face closely.

He turned towards her. 'When she came on her own but not when she brought him with her.'

'Him?'

'I'd rather keep his name out of it. She started going out with him two years before all this happened.'

'Somebody you didn't get on with.'

'He usually sat there ignoring me with his nose stuck in a magazine.'

'Was he with Liz the last time you saw her?'

'No, he sat outside in his car.'

'Did he have a problem with you?'

'He never said so but the funny part was when he turned up not long after I learned about Liz's body being found. I didn't expect to see him again and, looking back, I wish I hadn't.'

'What happened?'

'He was all smarmy nice, saying how upset he was when he heard about Liz. He gave me some money and told me to buy something with it.'

'What did you think?'

'Nothing at first; apart from seeing it as his way of making up for all the times he'd ignored me. What I didn't know was what he really had up his sleeve.'

'You saw him again?'

'He came back a few days later and took me out for a ride in his little two-seater which he'd never let me get near before. Then, another time, he took me to the pictures. Soon it became a regular treat – two or three times a week

– and, when I think back, I can see how clever he was at winning my trust.'

'How long did this go on for?'

'A month, six weeks – maybe more.'

'Something changed?'

Andy looked at her. His lip started to quiver. 'I'm sorry,' he said finally. 'After all these years I still find it hard to talk about.'

'Take your time,' said Jo.

Andy nodded. 'I'll be all right in a minute.'

Moon went over and fetched another round of drinks. Andy meanwhile sat with his fingers resting against his temples. 'Thanks,' he said when Moon put the fresh glass of lemonade down. The sound of the television grew louder. Somebody had just scored a goal.

'I suppose spending most of my life up to then in care didn't prepare me for what happened next,' Andy said when the shouting and cheering died down. 'He came along one day and said he was taking me to a party. It was about three weeks before Christmas and, before we went, he took me out shopping and bought me a new shirt and a new pair of trousers. I can remember feeling excited. I imagined there'd be music and people having fun.'

'Go on.'

'We went to this house in its own grounds where there were big flashy cars parked outside. It was then the mask he'd been wearing fell away. The pally, I'm your best mate stuff vanished and I can hear him now telling me to do whatever I was told to do when I got inside.'

'What did you say?'

'I think I must have sat there looking dumbstruck so, just to make the point, he laid it on thick. He said there were important people at the party, big noises who could make life difficult for me if I got on the wrong side of them. How did I feel? Scared sums it up. I didn't know what was coming but I felt sure it wasn't going to be good. Yes, it's easy looking back and thinking I should have told him to get stuffed but you have to put yourself in my shoes to appreciate why I kept my mouth shut. What do I remember about the next two hours? A roomful of men where I was looked at like a piece of meat. Another room where four or five of them came in one after the other and did what they wanted.'

'What about Liz's boyfriend? Was he a participant?'

'No, he just stood there in the background.'

'Did he say anything to you afterwards?'

'Only when he dropped me off back at the children's home. He gave me a handful of fivers and told me I should think myself lucky. I can remember thinking it must have been his idea of a sick joke. I made twenty-five quid that night. Afterwards I stood under the shower until the water ran cold then went to bed crying.'

'Did he leave you alone after that?'

'It went on for about four years. How often did he come for me? It varied. Sometimes months went by. Other times he'd turn up two or three times a week.'

'Was there always money involved?'

'Whatever he happened to have in his wallet.'

'Why didn't you report it to somebody?'

'I was scared what he'd do to me. I saw too how I could get into trouble because I'd taken money for letting these men do what they liked. The feeling of worthlessness came later.'

'Was it always the same place you went back to? The house in its own grounds you described?'

'No, every time it was somewhere different.'

'What about the men? Were they always the same faces?'

'Some of them I recognised but I tried my hardest not to look at them. All I knew was what I'd been told. They were important people and it didn't pay to cross them.'

'How did it end?'

'I ran away from the home. I lived on the streets for a few years, sleeping in doorways, that sort of stuff. I expected him to come after me so I kept on the move – one town after another, never staying too long in one place.'

Jo spoke again. 'Apart from us, have you ever told anybody about what happened to you?'

Andy shook his head. 'I felt ashamed. I didn't want people to know what I'd done.'

'You've gone through life with this secret?'

'It's not something I've ever wanted to share.'

Moon edged his chair closer. 'Does the name Jake Morris mean anything to you? '

Andy put his glass down.

Moon continued. 'We're working on the theory he was linked in some way with your sister's death. Is that what you think too? Was he the man you've just described to us? Liz's boyfriend? With Liz out of the way did he come after you because he saw you were vulnerable? Did he see the chance to make some easy money and was that all that mattered to him?'

Outside the pub, the three of them stood in the rain.

'It took me years to get my life together,' Andy said. 'I drifted from job to job but, bit by bit, I managed to get myself settled. Working nights isn't a lot of fun but I've got used to it and the extra money comes in handy.'

'What do you do?' Moon asked.

'I'm a Tool Repairer,' Andy replied. 'It's a skill I picked up and, on nights, there's nobody in the Tool Room except me.'

'You prefer working on your own?'

'If I'm truthful I'm not much of a mixer – never had a steady girlfriend. I suppose these days I'd have an army of psychologists swarming all over me trying to sort my head out and, yes, what happened to me thirty years ago has cast a deep shadow over my life.'

They watched him as he walked off into the darkness, disappearing from sight as he went round a street corner: a lonely stooping figure in a wet donkey jacket on his way to clock in for another eight hour shift.

'Penny for your thoughts,' said Jo as they got back into the car. ' If this is true – if Morris had ties to a ring of paedophiles operating in the seventies and if the senior officer in charge of the investigation into Sharon Baxter's murder was a paedophile, isn't this the connection you've been looking for? The reason the police didn't go after Morris and pinned Sharon's murder on an innocent man instead? Protecting him was their way of protecting themselves?'

'You may be right, Jo.'

'But what?'

'We need evidence to link Morris with Sid Marples and so far we haven't got any. Asking Andy Woodall to pick out Sid Marples as one of the men who abused him is a tall order when Sid is dead. There are probably some old photographs of him lying around somewhere but, even if Andy recognised him, an identification based on a child's recollection of what he saw thirty years ago isn't going to cut much ice. Then don't forget the evidence linking Sid Marples to a ring of paedophiles rests on what Alf Stepney told me in strict confidence.'

'So what are you saying? After all this we've run up against a brick wall?'

'It could be.'

'Or what?'

'Search me, Jo. I wish I knew.'

It was just after eight when Moon dropped Jo back at her apartment.

'You could walk away from this Charlie,' she said as she gathered her belongings together. 'You've got a career, a family to support. I'd be the first to understand why you wouldn't want to risk everything on what could still turn out to be a dead end.'

'What do you think, Jo?'

'What I think doesn't matter. I don't stand in your shoes.'

CHAPTER NINE

THE BUG

WILLOUGHBY'S ROUTINE WAS TO SPEND THE FIRST hour of every day clearing his desk. Moon had been slotted in for half past eleven – an indicator, perhaps, of where he ranked on the Team Penda Commander's list of priorities.

Stopping off in the gents to straighten his tie, he made his way to the foot of the open staircase which took him up two flights to the top corridor. This corridor and the long walk to Willoughby's office at the end always brought back unpleasant memories. The sound of his feet padding on the carpet tiles, the smell of furniture polish, the water cooler set back in its alcove, the uneasy brooding silence all helped to remind him of the occasions he'd been summoned here in the past. This time, however, it was he, Moon, who had asked for the meeting; he, Moon, who had spent most of the morning rehearsing what he was going to say.

'Come'. It was Willoughby's usual answer to a knock on the door – cold, unwelcoming and adenoidal. Moon entered to find him sitting at his desk in the act of what looked like signing letters.

'Can we make this quick?' he said not looking up and pointing with the end of his pen to the chair standing in an acre of space in front of his desk where he was indicating Moon should sit.

Moon did as he was told but moved the chair to bring it closer. 'Thank you for making the time to see me, sir,' he began in a voice which gave no hint of what was coming.

'Well, what is it? My schedule today is tight as it is.'

'You will recall the conversation we had earlier in the year, sir. The one where you asked me to make sure in future I brought any matters to your attention which may have a bearing on the reputation of the Team.'

'What of it?'

'Something has come up. Something I feel you ought to know about.'

Moon spent the next five minutes going over the story told to him by Denny Wilbur. Willoughby stopped signing his letters. White pre-apoplectic patches had started to appear on his cheeks. Finally he could contain himself no longer.

'Hold it there, Charlie. You're telling me you sat and listened to this ridiculous story? This man Wilbur is a notorious criminal. All sorts of alarm bells should have been going off in your head.'

'Yes, sir, they did.'

'So I hope you're going to tell me you reported this conversation to the prison authorities and asked them to deal with it. A prisoner hanging himself in his cell and anything related to it is their business.'

'With respect, sir, I beg to differ.'

'What?'

'If the allegations are true we're looking at how an innocent man came to be convicted of murder. The man in question was arrested and put before the court by members of this force – which seems to make it our business, wouldn't you say?'

Willoughby bristled. 'I've never heard such nonsense. The 'if' in this case is a big 'if'. Wilbur has a track record going back many years of lying his way out of countless criminal charges. He's the past master of deceit. What claim does somebody like him have to getting the world outside the walls of Winson Green Prison to believe what he says? It needs to be made clear that West Midlands Police will have no further truck with him.'

'Again with respect, sir, that may not be such a good idea.'

'And why not?'

'Denny Wilbur may be all the things you've said but he's been around the block enough times to know how to get his voice heard. The word back from me that we're not going to take another look at what happened in 1978 will push him into exploring what other avenues are open to him. He could write to his MP but don't forget we're talking about somebody who is well connected and won't hesitate to pull a few strings if he has to. On top of which, when it comes out he raised his concerns with a senior police officer – namely me – it won't look good if all we did was sit on our hands. An innocent man sent down for life, the potential of a killer still on the loose – we'll be struggling to keep the image of the Team intact. Don't you agree, sir?'

Willoughby blinked. For the first time in all the years Moon had known him he looked lost for words. Moon guessed the ramifications of what he'd just heard were slowly sinking in – but Willoughby wasn't done yet.

'Don't think you're backing me into a corner,' he snapped angrily. 'I know what you're angling for and, before you suggest it, let me make it crystal clear there's no way I would ever let an officer with your dismal record anywhere near an investigation which could come under scrutiny from people I have to answer to. If a review of this case is called for, I'll recommend it's carried out by another force so impartiality can be seen to be observed.'

'There's something else you need to know, sir. The senior officer in charge of the investigation back in 1978 was Detective Chief Inspector Marples – he was a little before my time but I take it the name will be familiar to you.'

Willoughby blinked again. All trace of his usual icy demeanour had vaporised. 'What the devil are you driving at?' he blazed, leaning forward over his desk with his fists clenched.

'Nothing, sir. I never had anything to do with Detective Chief Inspector Marples but I understand there were rumours circulating about the way he went about his business.'

'Such as what?'

'I don't know but I would suggest we need to be careful about inviting another force to go over what Detective

Chief Inspector Marples got up to years ago. You never know what might come out.'

This hit the raw nerve. Willoughby sat back with an ashen look on his face.

'Unless you've got any further questions, sir, I'll get out of your hair,' Moon said as he stood up to go. 'We can talk another time perhaps. When your schedule isn't so tight.'

• • •

'I left him to sweat,' said Moon as Jo and he sat down in a quiet corner of the city centre pub where they'd met before.

Jo looked puzzled. 'Is this clever thinking on your part, Charlie Moon? In which case, you'll have to explain. After all wasn't the idea to keep Willoughby in the dark until you'd got a few more facts up your sleeve? As it is he could just take you off the case. Wouldn't he be happier with somebody like Millership who could be relied on not to rock the boat?'

'I'm sure he would but he knows one false move on his part brings in the risk of me blowing the whistle on him. I've got him by the balls and he knows it. The look on his face said everything.'

'Hang on a minute, Charlie, are you suggesting Willoughby knew about this man Marples and did nothing?'

'Don't get me wrong, Jo, I recognise he inherited a bad situation when he took over and he must have been faced with some stark choices. Sid Marples may have disappeared from the scene but the rumours about him must have been pretty thick on the ground. Willoughby would have had to pick between bringing him back from London to face the music or letting sleeping dogs lie.'

Jo frowned. 'If what you're saying is true, I still don't understand why somebody in Willoughby's position – somebody who was brought in to clean up – took the decision not to do anything.'

'Don't you?'

'Stop talking in riddles, Charlie. It's one of your more annoying habits. Explain why Willoughby would have turned a blind eye to crimes against children.'

'To understand Willoughby, you have to understand how his mind works. He instinctively backs away from anything which could end up as headlines in the papers. In the case of Sid Marples he'd see straight away he'd be taking on a big beast with friends in high places and influential connections. Most of all, he'd see the threat to himself and that would be enough to give him cold feet.'

'Phew, Charlie, this gets more complicated by the minute. Are you really prepared to take this all the way?'

'If I have to but, when you think about it, what I have I got to lose? Willoughby has had my card marked for the past two years. He's only waiting for the right opportunity to come along to have me put out to grass. Doing this my way means, if I go down, I take him with me.'

'You're not losing sight of what this is all about? The poor innocent who went to jail because nobody would stick up for him? We're looking at bigger issues here than the private battle between you and Willoughby.'

'I couldn't agree more, Jo. At the end of the day who could give a toss about what happens to Willoughby or, for that matter, me? We both fade into utter insignificance when it comes to the people whose lives have been ruined. Sanctimonious though it sounds, they're the ones who need justice and, in the absence of anybody else, perhaps it falls on me to make sure they get it.'

• • •

'It's a relief all this is out in the open,' said Thompson after Moon finished filling him in on the meeting with Willoughby. 'What I don't see, though, is where it leaves us.'

'Neither do I,' said Moon. 'But from here on this is going to be down to just me.'

Thompson frowned. 'I don't understand,' he said

'You heard,' said Moon. 'You, Scotty and Tambo detach yourself from this inquiry. Anything you've done up to now you can say you acted on my instructions. Mr Willoughby may be in the picture but, if my guess is right, he won't pull the punches when it comes to laying traps.'

'I still don't understand,' said Thompson. 'As far as I'm concerned, I'm happy to stand shoulder to shoulder with you and I'm sure Scotty and Tambo would feel the same way.'

'Dave, Willoughby wouldn't think twice about having the three of you removed from the Team but, with me, he'd have to justify his actions to people above him. Right now, I'm guessing the last thing he'd want is the top brass coming down here and poking their noses into what this is about?'

'All the same, Guv, I'm not happy about leaving you with the job of seeing this through on your own.'

'I appreciate your loyalty, Dave, but I know the risks I'm taking and, if it makes sense, it'll be a lot easier without the worry of what might happen to you, Scotty and Tambo weighing on my mind.'

• • •

Next morning Moon arrived at HQ early and took a short cut into his office via the fire door somebody had left open again. Stopping off in the kitchen to grab a cup of coffee, he made it his first job of the day to check his emails half-expecting to find something from Willoughby as it was not unusual for the Team Penda Commander to fire off edicts from his laptop computer in the middle of the night. Breathing a sigh of relief when he saw there was nothing, he settled down to dealing with the pile of paperwork which had built up on his desk over the last couple of days. As he sat there, however, he noticed something. A whiff in the air so faint it almost didn't register. A mix of tobacco and stale sweat, a smell which didn't belong but which was definitely there.

Moon put his coffee cup down and looked round. The three drawer filing cabinet, the coat hook on the back of the door, the waste paper basket over in the corner, the slats of the blinds which were in need of dusting: his eyes drifted down to the skirting board where they stopped. A length of standard electrical trunking running along the wall and fitted so flush it was scarcely noticeable – a length of extruded white plastic he couldn't remember seeing before.

Feeling his pulse quicken, he got up and went over to take a closer look. At one end the trunking connected to the junction box which served to carry the wiring to the phones and computer. At the other, it continued along the skirting disappearing finally into where the pipes to the central heating system had been boxed in. He dropped down onto his haunches. A small louvred grille had been screwed to the woodwork, white so it blended in perfectly, but traces of sawdust on the floor underneath gave away that somebody had fitted it recently. Somebody who had the smell of cigarettes and sweat on their clothes.

Moon went over to his desk where he kept a small set of screwdrivers. Selecting one which looked to be the right size, he took the precaution of locking the office door before getting down on his knees. The four small screws holding the grille in place came out easily revealing where somebody had cut a jagged hole in the wood with a jigsaw. Lying flat on his side, Moon angled his head so he could see inside the hole although he'd already guessed what he was going to find.

A tiny listening device of a type he'd seen used countless times by surveillance teams and the whole job looking like it had been done in a rush – somebody in such a hurry they hadn't even bothered to sweep up. He screwed the grille back carefully then stood up and brushed the dust from his trousers. A few seconds later he was making his way to the front desk where he found Sergeant Hobbs on duty.

'Anything going on, Mick?' he said casually picking up Sergeant Hobbs' newspaper and flicking through it.

'Not to my knowledge,' Sergeant Hobbs replied.

'A little bird told me we had some activity on site late last night.'

'That would be the people from IT doing a survey for the new computer system. All had to be done out of hours apparently. By order of DI Millership.'

'Fancy that,' said Moon casting his eyes over the sports pages. 'I didn't know anything about a new computer system. Still, I'm usually to last to find out anything when it comes to this high-tech stuff.'

'Join the club,' Sergeant Hobbs replied.

• • •

Later in the morning Moon sent Thompson a text message to arrange to meet at a tea stall in a lay-by which was one of their regular stopping off points when they were out together on a job. It was shortly after two when Moon drove up. Thompson was already standing outside his car with his hands thrust deep in the pockets of his bright yellow ski jacket.

'In your shoes I'd feel livid,' said Thompson when he'd listened to what Moon had to say about the hidden mike.

Moon shrugged. 'Getting angry won't help, Dave.'

Thompson nodded. 'I'll put Scotty and Tambo in the picture,' he said. 'Does the order for us to stay out of this still stand?'

'I think so – for the time being you'll just have to trust my judgment on what's best.'

After he watched Thompson drive off, Moon sat for a while taking note of the activity in the lay-by. Truckers swigging mugs of tea and chomping bacon sandwiches before getting back into their cabs and checking their tachographs. Weary motorists pulling in to get their heads down for ten minutes before continuing on their journeys.

Not feeling he wanted to go back to an office where one of Millership's snoops would be listening in to everything, he headed off in the opposite direction. At first he drove round randomly paying little attention to where he was going, coming to a set of temporary traffic lights at a road works where he sat waiting for them to change. JCM Litigation, personal injury specialists: it was only half a mile to the address Thompson had written down. He took the next left turn which brought him to a busy High Street where a butcher, a hairdresser and a dry cleaners caught his eye as he drove along in a queue of traffic. He checked the names on the shop fronts, crawling slowly behind a bus, until he came to the one he was looking for. A large sign in the window advertising guaranteed 100% compensation and the promise of no win, no fee. He pulled over into a line of parked cars where he sat with the engine idling. It all looked perfectly normal but, as he pondered on the dark mind behind this veneer of respectability, his eyes drifted to an MGB circa early sixties vintage painted in British Racing Green and parked against the kerb with its chromework gleaming in the late afternoon sun.

Still with no yearning to go back to the office, he decided to take a look at the other address Thompson had given him – the place out in the stockbroker belt where

Morris and his wife had lived for the last twenty years. With the daylight already starting to fade he drove another three miles to where the busy streets gave way to green fields. He stopped a few times to check the road map but, even so, he still almost managed to miss the turn. A lane which skirted the edge of a golf course where gorse bushes and clumps of silver birch grew between the greens and the fairways. Finally he came to a scattering of dwellings on the left hand side where he picked out the one he was looking for. A large detached house set back from the lane where there was room on the grass verge to pull over but instead of stopping he kept going not wishing to attract the attention of anybody who may have been watching from inside.

• • •

The streetlights were coming on as he drove back into the city. He rang Jo from the roof of a multi-storey car park and arranged to meet her for coffee.

'Bugging your office sounds like taking it to the extreme,' she said as they sat sipping Americanos in a place Jo chose because it was hidden away in a quiet backstreet. 'You're sure you're still up for this?'

'As sure as I'll ever be.'

'Charlie, I've been thinking, if this ring of paedophiles was operating as long ago as the seventies, a lot of children must have passed through their hands; children who are now grown up and capable of speaking out for themselves.'

'You're thinking exactly what I've thought – over all the years why has nobody come forward and said something? The answer could lie in what Andy Woodall told us about feeling ashamed of what they'd done or, alternatively, perhaps the victims kept quiet because they thought nobody would listen to them. It would be their word against people who were pillars of the community. You have to remember too Morris wouldn't have been above throwing in a few threats of violence if he thought anybody was getting ideas above their station about reporting him. Then I suppose you have to ask yourself what would have happened if somebody had plucked up the courage to go the police. Case referred to Detective Chief Inspector Marples or Detective Superintendent Marples as he later became? It scarcely bears thinking about.'

• • •

The next morning, thanks to a hold-up in the traffic, Moon arrived at HQ later than normal. It was quarter to nine according to the digital clock on the dashboard.

'I've got a message for you,' said Sergeant Hobbs as he spotted Moon walking past the front desk. 'DI Millership is after a word urgently. He said he tried ringing you on your mobile yesterday afternoon but you must have had it switched off.'

Moon made no comment, mainly because of the standing instruction Willoughby had given him two years before about keeping his phone on at all times. Already going through his mind though was why Millership wanted to see him. He guessed it was to do with the conversation he'd had with Willoughby and, as it turned out, he was right.

'Charlie,' said Millership when Moon walked in his office without knocking. 'Thanks for stopping by – I hope I've not dragged you away from anything important but the Boss was keen for us to get together as soon as possible.'

Moon said nothing. He studied Millership's gold cuff links and neatly clipped finger nails. This was damage limitation. Millership given the job of putting the genie back in the bottle and making sure it stayed there.

'You and I haven't always seen eye to eye,' Millership started by saying. 'We've crossed swords a few times over the years but I'd like to think we can be frank with one another.'

Moon still said nothing. He was waiting to see where this was leading.

'We don't live in an ideal world,' Millership continued. 'Sometimes tough decisions have to be made on where to draw the line under the past. Can I come to the point?'

'Please do.'

'Things went on years ago. Things you and I know about. Things which shouldn't have gone on but we need to think carefully before we start raking them up again.'

'I'm sorry, you'll have to explain,' said Moon maintaining a blank expression.

'Even if it relates to something which happened thirty years ago, a corruption allegation against a former senior officer would start off a big witch-hunt.'

'You're saying that would be bad?'

'I'm saying it would lead to everything and everybody coming under scrutiny. Nobody would know where it might finish up?'

'So what are you suggesting?'

Millership lowered his voice. 'This is off the record, Charlie. Never to be repeated, you understand? We get the conviction of the chappie who hung himself quashed on grounds which won't make it look like he was stitched up. We give Denny Wilbur the result he's after without bringing a police complaints investigation team down on our heads.'

'You're forgetting something. Whoever killed the girl is still out there. We would still be left with an unsolved murder on our hands.'

'But going back all those years would be an impossible job. Besides there were no other suspects so we wouldn't have a clue where to start.'

'Where do I come in?'

'I'm sorry...'

'Me – the fall guy if this convoluted conspiracy to pervert the course of justice you've just outlined collapses in a heap? Would Mr Willoughby and you be falling over yourselves in the rush to come to my rescue? I think not and so, if you don't mind, I'd rather we stopped this conversation right here. No doubt you'll be reporting back to Mr Willoughby. Let's hope what you tell him doesn't spoil his Christmas.'

CHAPTER TEN

THE BIKER

Cathy took the girls to see a Panto on Saturday leaving Moon with the afternoon free to himself. There were any number of jobs he could have done around the house – a washer on the kitchen tap which needed changing; a loose tile in the shower room which wanted fixing back on – but, instead of chalking up a few brownie points on the domestic front, he found himself getting in the car and driving once again to the lane which went past the golf course. The journey took him forty minutes with a few flurries of sleet in the air as he came once more to the scattering of houses and finally to the one he was looking for. He glanced at it as he went by but didn't slow down. A quarter of a mile further on he came to where the lane passed into woodland and there he saw what he'd seen the first time he came this way. A clearing on the left with a few picnic tables dotted among the trees and a hard standing at the side of the lane where cars could park. He pulled over and switched off the engine. There was no one around and, putting two and two together, he guessed the weather had put anybody off who may have been having ideas about going for a Saturday afternoon stroll in the woods.

Getting out of the car, he went round to the boot and retrieved the pair of wellingtons he kept there along with the old anorak he wore at weekends. He checked his watch. It was quarter to two which gave him a good hour of daylight left.

From the clearing he could see a number of footpaths going off into the trees. He took a few seconds to get his bearings before setting off. The trees, he saw, were a mix of silver birch and alder interspersed with holly bushes. The sleet had almost stopped but a cold wind had got up which hadn't been there earlier. The path he'd taken climbed steeply to an outcrop of sandstone where he could look out over the treetops. He could see the golf course in the distance with the flags on the greens fluttering in the breeze while, over to the west, the sun showed briefly between dark bands of clouds. He wondered if he would be able to get a view of Morris's property from up here but he was disappointed and came to the conclusion it must be hidden in a dip.

He turned to look the other way – to where, beyond the trees, the land kept rising up a steep bank covered in gorse bushes and rabbit paths. At the top of the bank stood a row of tall conifers, the species impossible to make out at this distance, but, just as he was thinking of retracing his steps back to the car, something made him stop. Up in the conifers the last rays of the setting sun briefly caught on something. It was there and it was gone again but he had no doubt about what he'd seen. The light reflecting off the lenses of a pair of binoculars. Somebody up there was watching him.

• • •

'What did you make of it?' Jo asked when Moon next spoke to her on the phone. It was Monday morning and he was sitting in the car on the piece of derelict land overlooking the railway lines where he'd come to get away.

'I'm not sure,' he replied. 'We could be looking at a perfectly innocent explanation like somebody out birdwatching.'

'I thought you said it was getting dark.'

'It was.'

'You don't think it could be Willoughby or Millership up to their old tricks and keeping an eye on you to see what you get up to on your day off?'

'Nobody knew where I was going on Saturday afternoon. I only decided myself at the last minute.'

'Nobody followed you?'

'I kept a careful check in the mirrors. I always do.'

'So what's going on?'

'Search me, Jo, but, if we are talking about surveillance, one thought which did cross my mind is the target may not be me. I'd need to check this out but I'd say whoever was standing in those trees had a bird's-eye view over the back of Morris's house.'

'I'm not getting my head round this, Charlie.'

'Nor me – except for the possibility somebody else may have taken an interest in him and I just happened to come along.'

'Like who?'

'That's what I need to find out. What we can't rule out, though, is Morris could be on somebody else's watch list.'

After ending the call to Jo, Moon adjusted his seat to bring it back into the upright position. He knew he had things to do back at the office but he felt no inclination to be spending the rest of the day staring at one spreadsheet after the next.

He started the engine. Three quarters of an hour later he found himself back at the picnic place where, just like before, there was nobody to be seen. He changed into his wellingtons again then set off on the path he'd taken on Saturday afternoon coming to where the view of the golf course opened up in front of him. It was a day when a grey winter mist hung over everything and there was no wind so the flags on the greens drooped limply in the damp air. He turned to look the other way – towards the steep bank where the conifer trees at the top were hidden in a blanket of low cloud. He took a deep breath. Soon he was making his way through the gorse bushes feeling the burs catching against his sleeves and noticing the tiny droplets of water clinging to the spiders' webs. The climb up the bank was getting steeper. Once or twice he slipped. Once or twice he managed to regain his footing. Half way up he tripped over a bramble and sent a shower of loose stones cascading down the slope. He looked up. He could make out the shapes of the conifers shrouded in mist but then fleetingly he thought he saw something move. A trick of the light perhaps or a large bird up in the trees startled by the noise of the miniature landslide he'd set off? He kept his eyes glued to the spot. Five seconds, ten seconds passed then, without warning, a figure dressed in black broke cover and started running.

With his heart pounding, Moon scrambled up the last few yards of the slope where he arrived just in time to see the figure making off through the trees. He gave chase but quickly realised his wellingtons weren't made for running. Beyond the conifers he came out onto a wide track along which he spotted the figure sprinting off into the distance but it hadn't gone far before it veered off to the left into a clump of bushes. At first Moon was puzzled but then he heard the unmistakable sound of an engine starting up and, seconds later, a motorbike shot out of the bushes with the mysterious figure in black sitting astride it.

Moon stopped running. As he stood catching his breath he watched the motorbike speed off into the distance where he soon lost sight of it. He listened to the noise of its exhausts gradually getting fainter and fainter until finally he could no longer hear them.

Anybody who knew Charlie Moon knew he'd spent a large part of his boyhood days standing on station platforms writing down engine numbers. It was hardly surprising therefore that he quickly worked out that the track on which he now stood was what remained of an old railway line. Nature was slowly encroaching back on where trains had once run and, as he stood there, Moon hazarded a guess the lines had been lifted at some time in the fifties or sixties. A little further on, he could see a stack of old wooden sleepers half-hidden in the weeds where they'd been forgotten and left behind by some long-departed demolition gang.

He looked back at the conifers. A screen of Scots pines planted there no doubt by some landowner back in Victorian times to stop the sight of passing trains spoiling his view of the countryside. Slowly he retraced his steps through the trees, following the trail of scuff marks made by his wellingtons on the carpet of fallen cones and pine needles. The damp air was filled with the sharp scent of resin and the only sound, apart from the snapping of twigs under his feet, was the steady drip, drip, drip of water droplets coming down from the branches. Finally he came to the place where he'd first seen the figure in black – a place where the undergrowth had been trampled and somebody had dropped a can. Below where he stood the land fell away sharply down the steep bank onto the grey scene beneath. As he stood there, though, the mist parted for just long enough to reveal what he suspected all along. A view overlooking the house where Morris and his wife lived. Somebody who had just ridden off on a motorbike had chosen the perfect place for spying on what went on down there.

• • •

That evening Moon's offer to help the girls with their homework didn't go the way he hoped. The homework in question turned out to be Computer Studies and Moon, the complete IT illiterate, soon found himself floundering. It ended with the girls giving him a lesson and, after a while, he retreated to the box room upstairs which doubled as a home office. He took with him an old one-inch Ordnance Survey map he'd dug out of the back of a drawer earlier. The map – original price four shillings and sixpence – had been published in 1953 and belonged to his father who once cherished a short-lived and largely unrealised ambition to take the family out for walks in the country at weekends. It showed the area around the city as it looked fifty years ago and, from picking out familiar features and place names, he quickly found what he was looking for. The railway line was shown as still open and after tracing his finger along it, he came to where the plantation of conifer trees was clearly marked. The golf course was also shown but there were no houses along the lane leading him to form the view they weren't there when the map was drawn. The purpose of the exercise, though, wasn't to indulge his fascination with old maps but to see where the railway line went to and how somebody riding a motorbike would be able to access it. A mile or so beyond where he'd seen the figure in black disappearing into the mist he came to what he was looking for. A bridge where the railway once crossed a minor road at a point where a small station was shown.

He folded the map away. Later he put it with the rest of the things he planned to take with him in the morning.

• • •

It was a cold and frosty start to Tuesday and, before setting off, Moon had to spend five minutes scraping ice from the windscreen of the car. His journey was one he'd planned carefully. It took him along quiet back roads pitted with frozen potholes while, over to the east, a big red sun was starting to come up. He drove for the best part of an hour coming finally to the place he'd found on his father's old map where he saw straight away the bridge that once carried the railway line over the road was no longer there. Instead all that remained were the truncated spurs of an embankment supported by crumbling retaining walls. At the side of the road was an open space where a heap of worn tyres had been dumped. Here Moon pulled over to take a look round quickly working out that this was where the station had once stood before it had been reduced to the pile of rubble he could see sticking out of what was left of last summer's weeds.

At other times Moon would have spent hours poring over a place like this searching for odd bits of railway memorabilia but today he had more pressing things on his mind. He parked the car behind an overgrown buddleia bush where it couldn't be seen by anybody passing by on the road then, with his wellingtons and his old anorak back on again, he set off walking.

Out in the fresh morning air he noticed there was still a thick rime of frost coating blades of grass in places where the sun hadn't reached while the track bed of the old railway line looked well-trodden showing at least somebody still used it. As he walked along he noticed tyre tracks in the frozen mud including some that looked like they'd been made recently.

Soon he was passing between empty fields while, up above, there was scarcely a cloud in the sky apart from a few wisps of cirrus. He strode along with his hands in his pockets coming to where the old railway line passed through a cutting as its course crossed from one valley to the next. Here bare sandstone rock faces looked down on him as he plodded along to the hollow echo of his own footsteps and the chatter of jackdaws from the crags above.

Emerging from the cutting back into the sunshine, he paused briefly to get his bearings. Ahead the track curved away into the distance following the contours of the hillside. He spotted the conifers about a quarter of a mile away and, closer to, the stack of old railway sleepers. He set off again, advancing more cautiously this time, not knowing what to expect. He came to the sleepers where he paused briefly to take a look at them. A few yards further on was the clump of bushes and the place the mysterious figure in black had used as a hiding place for his motorbike. One step at a time, he kept his eyes glued on the clump of bushes seeing as he drew closer that they were a ragged mix of stunted hawthorns and elderberries. Then he saw it. The motorbike with the bright winter sunshine reflecting off its chrome and its front wheel pushed into the thick tangle of undergrowth. He noticed there were two panniers on the sides and what looked like a waterproof groundsheet strapped to the pillion but, as he stood there, he heard a sound which made his blood turn cold. The soft crunch of somebody's boots. A sound coming from behind.

CHAPTER ELEVEN

UNFINISHED BUSINESS

MOON TURNED SLOWLY. THE FIGURE IN BLACK WAS just a few feet away wearing a crash helmet with the visor pulled down. Moon tensed, sensing the stand-off but then the figure reached up and, with a twist of the head, removed the helmet to reveal a face Moon immediately recognised. A face with a ghostly pallor and a receding hairline. Andy Woodall, last seen as he disappeared round a street corner in a wet donkey jacket on his way to clock on for another eight hour night shift.

'I knew it was you, Inspector,' he smiled. 'I didn't expect to come across you creeping up behind me but I was sure it wouldn't be long before I bumped into you again. What am I doing here? That's what you want to know, isn't it? Could it be some crazy mixed-up idea I've been thinking up for getting my own back on the man who cast such a dark shadow over my life?'

'You tell me,' said Moon shifting his position so the sun was no longer in his eyes. 'I'd be the first to agree you've had it tough and nobody could blame you for wanting to get even but taking the law into your own hands isn't the answer.'

'You don't get it,' said Andy. 'If I'd wanted to put a dent in his skull with a baseball bat I could have done it a long time ago.'

'So what's this about? If you're not scheming to punch Morris's lights out, explain what you're doing standing up here in all weathers.'

'It's a free country. There's no law against being out in the fresh air.'

'Don't fuck me about. We both know the score. I can play hardball if I want to.'

Andy smiled again. 'I don't scare easily, Inspector. I go back thirty years with Jake Morris so I think I've earned the right to come and see for myself how he's profited from his misspent life. I found out where he lives back in the summer. Once I put my mind to it, it didn't take me long to track him down and working nights gives me free time during the day to do as I please. I answer to nobody. Not even you.'

'All the same don't expect me to buy the idea you're up here just to fill in a few hours before you go to work. Something's bugging you and we'll waste a lot less of one another's time if you tell me what it is.'

'It's a long story,' said Andy. 'Bits of it you know. Other bits you don't. It's up to you whether you want to hear it or not.'

'I'm listening,' said Moon. 'Don't try to pull the wool over my eyes, that's all.'

Andy took a deep breath. 'It goes back to when my mother passed away,' he began. 'She'd been in a hospice for three months but I hadn't seen her since I was little so I didn't know she was ill. One morning when I got back from work there was a message to say she wanted to see me. It seems somebody from Social Services had found out where I lived. We're talking about twelve months ago. I didn't know what to think. '

'You went?'

'My bike was off the road at the time and the only way I could get there was on three buses. When I arrived I was shown into this room where a frail looking woman I scarcely recognised was lying in a bed propped up by pillows. It was hard to know what to say after so long and she must have found it as difficult as I did. She thanked me for coming. She said she realised what a mess she'd made of her life but it was too late now to change anything.'

'So why did she ask to see you?'

'She said she wanted to say she was sorry. She hoped one day I'd find it in my heart to forgive her.'

'Was that it?'

'Not quite. She told me she knew she didn't have long to live but there was still some unfinished business. She meant Liz and what happened to her. She didn't believe what she'd been told about Liz's death being accidental. She knew Liz kept bad company and deep down she blamed herself for not being there when she started to stray off the straight and narrow.'

'Are you saying your mother knew about Morris?'

'I didn't ask her. Perhaps I should have done but I didn't.'

'What else did she have to say about Liz?'

'She identified the body – which I didn't know. The police took her to a mortuary somewhere near to the beach where she was found.'

'You're telling me your mother was handing over the job of getting to the bottom of what happened to Liz – was that the unfinished business?'

'She told me about the place in Worcester where Liz had gone to live. It was my mother who gave me the name of the lady who used to run it and her address. Don't ask me how she came to have it because I don't know. What she did say though was she was going to get in touch with her but she hadn't got round to it. Sadly, not getting round to things was my mother all over.'

'How did you leave it with her?'

'I promised I'd do my best. What I didn't tell her was I also had unfinished business.'

'By which you meant unfinished business with Morris?'

Andy didn't answer.

'So you wrote to Alice Cobb,' Moon continued. 'You found though she wasn't able to help you with what you really wanted to know.'

'There's more,' said Andy. 'Two weeks after I went to see my mother I got a phone call from the hospice to say she'd taken a turn for the worse. I got there as quickly as I could but, when I arrived, it was too late. She went peacefully, so I was told. Then, after the funeral, I booked a week off work which went down officially as bereavement leave. I didn't tell anybody where I was going. I set off down the motorway on my bike. I remember the weather was freezing cold and it took hours to reach the coast. Fortunately for me it was out of season so I had no problem finding a B&B with vacancies. I spent the week going in pubs chatting to the locals in the hope I'd find somebody who could shed some light on how Liz's body came to be in the sea.'

'Did you have any joy?'

'Not at first – then, one evening, as I was sitting having a pint, a character who wouldn't give me his name came over and started talking. He said he'd heard I'd been asking questions about the drowned girl and wanted to know if I was anything to do with the police. When I explained who I was he said he thought I might be interested in what he had to say. He told me he used to be a coast guard and how, a few days before Liz's body was found, a holidaymaker out walking on a lonely stretch of the coast path reported something he'd seen.'

CHAPTER TWELVE

INTERLUDE
THE BIRDWATCHER

SEPTEMBER 1971

HE SAT DOWN ON THE HIGHEST PART OF THE BEACH to eat his sandwiches. In front of him the pebbles sloped away to the shoreline in a series of terraces marking where the tides came in and went out. Down by the water's edge a group of sanderlings darted backwards and forwards picking out small creatures thrown up on a patch of fine shingle by the incoming waves. The sea was rough today, driven by a cold onshore wind which battered his ears and drowned out all other sounds while, even this far back, he felt the wet of salt spray on his face.

The short break before term started was a last minute thing. The chance to spend a few days on his own catching up on reading and watching migrating sea birds and waders making their way south for the winter. He came prepared for all weathers – warm clothes and waterproofs for rainy days, shorts and tee shirts for when the sun came out. It was space – a time to relax, unwind and put daily cares to one side.

Not in any hurry to set off walking again, he took his time finishing his sandwiches and carried on watching the sanderlings with their matchstick legs scurrying first one way then the other. Higher up the beach a carrion crow foraged among the blackened strands of bladderwrack while a herring gull hovered overhead balancing on the wind and looking for its next meal among the trash of plastic bottles, discarded fishing lines and tattered bin-liners. He took the pair of binoculars he always carried out of his rucksack and raised them to his eyes to take a closer look at the sanderlings as they moved further up the beach. Briefly he caught sight of something in the surf which could have been a grey seal and he kept the binoculars trained on the spot but the seal, if it was one, didn't reappear.

When the sanderlings were too far away, he shifted the angle of his position slightly so he could study the view along the coast in the direction his walk was taking him in. Broken wooden pallets jettisoned from cargo ships and tree trunks bleached by the sun and sea littered the foreshore where they had been cast up by winter storms. Behind the beach, the marshy wetland where harriers swooped over the reed-beds and wildfowl gathered to feed on the brackish pools. He followed the line of the shore to where it faded into a haze of mist and sea spray. There, in the distance, he picked out a spit of land jutting into the sea but, whether it was man-made or a natural feature, was impossible to tell at this range. He adjusted the binoculars to bring it into closer focus. It looked to be about half a mile away with waves breaking against it sending great shoots of water up into the air. But then he noticed something else. Somebody standing on the spit, a solitary figure, a girl dressed in black looking out to sea with what looked like a shawl or a blanket wrapped around her shoulders. He strained his eyes to pick out more details. She had long hair which the wind whipped across her face but she never took her attention off the breakers as they rolled in one after the other.

He kept the binoculars trained on her as she stood there motionless. Something about her though struck him as troubled and, in the end, he put the binoculars down feeling he was intruding on somebody's private moment. The herring gull was still on patrol, the carrion crow still picking around in the seaweed but curiosity finally drove him to take another look at the figure standing on the narrow spit.

She was still there in exactly the same place where she'd been before. The tide was coming in, the waves getting bigger, the sea a turmoil of green water but then she turned so now she was looking back towards the land. In a second he saw why. A second figure was approaching, a man in dark clothing picking his way across the rocks and rough ground, finally stopping when he came to within a few feet of where she stood. A pair of trippers on a day out at the seaside? One telling the other not to stand so close to the water's edge? They looked to be locked in conversation yet something about them made him keep watching. A foreboding. A feeling of something about to happen and then, without warning, she tried to push past him to which the man reacted by grabbing her by the arms. For several seconds they struggled with one another, tugging and pulling, but, just as it looked she might break free from his grip, he seized her bodily, lifted her up off her feet and threw her into the sea just as an enormous wave came crashing in.

It was all over in a flash. Still with his binoculars focussed on where he'd last seen her, he noticed something black floating on the surface of the water and realised it was her shawl. Only a strong swimmer would have been able to make it back to land and he saw straight away the odds were on her being caught in a current and swept out to sea. He turned his attention to the man who was still standing on the rocks gazing down into the water. For a few seconds it looked like he might do something but, in the end, he turned round and walked away. One last look over his shoulder then he was gone into the mist.

CHAPTER THIRTEEN

THE SCRAPYARD

'THE HOLIDAYMAKER RAN FOR HELP,' ANDY
continued. 'They sent out a lifeboat and a helicopter but,
after searching for hours, they found nothing so they put
it down to him being mistaken. The light when there's
a sea mist can play funny tricks on people who aren't
used to it or so he was told. It turned out, however, he
was a professor in physics from a university up north, an
amateur ornithologist, a credible witness, you might say.
Somebody who knew exactly what his eyes had seen.'

'So why did nobody connect this report with the
discovery of Liz's body? Why didn't the authorities have
the gumption to put two and two together?'

'Apparently all this happened ten miles further up the
coast from where Liz's body was washed up. Two different
lots of police were involved. A classic case of the right
hand not knowing what the left one was doing was the
way it was put to me.'

'So you're saying Liz's death may not have been an accident. She could have been the girl standing on the rocks. Morris could have been the man who threw her in the sea.'

A plane flew over. A tiny silver dot in the clear blue sky.

Andy spoke again. 'I want you to be straight with me, Inspector. No bullshit, you understand. I want to know where this is going. No, I'm not trying to poke my nose in where it's not welcome but this is important to me. How close are you to putting Morris in front of a jury?'

'No bullshit?'

'That's what I said.'

Moon took a deep breath. 'The case I'm investigating goes back many years and I knew from the start it would be a tough call digging into events the guilty parties have done their best to cover up. Am I any nearer to getting to the truth? I'm hopeful I'll get a breakthrough if I keep going long enough but I'm under no illusions I could be kidding myself. I've seen too many cases in the past where scum like Morris walk off scot-free. I'm a realist. I have to be. I wouldn't be doing the job I'm doing if I wasn't.'

Andy nodded. 'I've lived with injustice all my life. It's not easy but I've got used to it. Like you I keep hoping something good will come along but like you I'm also a realist.'

Moon gave Andy a card with his contact details on it then watched him as he got on his bike and rode off, seeing the last of him as he disappeared into the cutting. He stood for a while taking in the silence. There were a few more clouds in the sky and, further along the track, a pied wagtail picked among the stones.

He checked his watch. It was quarter past eleven and his thoughts turned to getting back to the car but, before setting off on the return leg of his walk, he decided to go and take a another look at the view from the other side of the conifers which were just a few yards from where he stood. This time he knew where he was going and, after ducking his head here and there to avoid low branches, he came once again to the top of the steep bank. Today the bright winter sun picked out everything in sharp detail and, as he stood there, his eyes fell once more on the house below with its neatly tended lawns and shrubberies. He studied the scene for several seconds taking in the ordinariness of it all then, just as he made to go, he saw something he hadn't noticed at first. In the back garden of the house the figure of a woman standing perfectly still. He waited to see if she moved but she didn't. She stayed in exactly the same position. A woman outside on a cold winter morning staring at nothing with her arms in the sleeves of her coat. She was still there when he turned and walked away.

• • •

Moon's first job when he got back to the car was to ring Thompson.

'Anything happening Dave?'

'Nothing we can't handle,' Thompson replied. 'Upstairs is all quiet if that's what you were wondering. No sign of Mr Willoughby or DI Millership all morning.'

After ending the call to Thompson he tapped in the string of numbers which connected him with Jo. When he finished filling her in on the unexpected encounter with Andy Woodall, he arranged to meet her for a drink later.

Moon's first thought as he reversed the car out of its hiding place behind the buddleia bush was to find somewhere to buy food. He drove off towards the city passing through a small village on the way where he stopped off at a bakery selling freshly-made sandwiches. Two miles further on he pulled into a lay-by where he sat eating with the window wound down. Over to his left, an empty playing field on the edge of a housing estate where a lone seagull sat perched on top of one of the goalposts stretching its wings. The seagull flew off as he got out of the car to brush the crumbs off his trousers.

Forty minutes later found him back at the crime scene standing on the bridge and looking down once more into the cutting where the canal and the railway line ran underneath. The road was busier at this time of day. Trucks laden with swarf and metal off cuts were making their way towards the scrapyard while, down below, a train went by – a three coach multiple unit rattling over a set of points as it headed into the city. He watched as a vee-shaped wake made its way across the canal and, seconds later, a brown rat climbed out of the water onto the bank and disappeared into the long grass.

He walked back slowly towards the car which he'd left on the same piece of spare ground where he'd left it before. In front of him the scrapyard where he could see the jib of a crane at work over the top of a rusty corrugated iron fence daubed with graffiti. A pick-up truck went by piled high with scrap metal and the three men sitting shoulder to shoulder inside turned to stare. Moon smiled to himself. Half the stuff on the back of the truck was probably pinched but little did the three men know that the stranger in the overcoat walking across the bridge was an officer of the law.

When he reached the car he paused by the door but, instead of getting in, he carried on walking in the direction of the scrapyard noticing, as he had done the first time, how the road beyond it came to an abrupt end in what looked like an abandoned landfill site.

Drawing level with the gate, he could see the pick-up truck with its brake lights on stopped by a weighbridge where the driver was in conversation with a man in a hard hat and high-vis vest. The pick-up moved off, going to where it had presumably been told to offload among the piles of battered old fridges and washing machines. The man in the hard hat looked across and saw Moon standing by the gate.

'Can I help you?' he called out over the noise of a giant metal crusher which was at work not far from where he stood. Moon walked towards him, waiting until he was just a few feet away before he reached into his inside pocket and brought out his ID.

'Who's in charge of this place?' said Moon casting his eyes around.

'That'll be me,' the man replied. 'The boss has taken himself off to Tenerife for a fortnight leaving muggins here to run everything while he's away.'

'Is there somewhere quiet we can talk?'

The man nodded and, after shouting across to one of his workmates to take over, he pointed Moon in the direction of an old caravan standing in one corner of the site with its tyres flat and propped up on bricks. Steel welded mesh panels had been stapled over the windows presumably as a measure to deter intruders. Once inside Moon quickly gathered the caravan doubled up as a mess room and a place where workers got changed. Lockers took up most of the wall space while two Formica-topped tables pushed together sat in the middle surrounded by a random collection of broken chairs. The man took his hard hat off and the heavy industrial gloves he was wearing. Without the hat, Moon saw his head was shaved and he wore a gold stud in one ear. He looked to be in his late forties but he could have been older.

'You worked here long?' said Moon continuing to look round.

'More years than I care to think,' the man replied. 'I was taken on by the boss's father after I left school.'

'Is the money good?'

The man grinned. 'Some weeks are better than others.'

'Let me take you back to the seventies,' said Moon pulling up a chair. 'The body of a girl found down by the canal. She'd been stabbed a number of times – does it ring any bells?'

'Why do you ask?'

'I'm thinking the police at the time must have gone over this place with a fine toothcomb. Right next to the scene of the crime, I imagine they turned it upside down looking for the missing murder weapon.'

'They didn't find anything if that's what you want to know. They looked for the best part of a week while we were told to stay away.'

'When did you hear they'd arrested somebody?'

'We were still laid-off when the word got round.'

'Did you know the man they charged?'

'They told us he worked at the hospital. They said he lived locally but none of the crew had heard of him.'

'What did you think?'

'What I've always thought. They got the wrong man.'

'You seem pretty certain.'

The metal crusher stopped working.

'This all happened a long time ago,' said the man after the silence had gone on for a while.

'Tell me about it.'

The man came over and joined Moon sitting at the table pushing an ashtray filled with nub ends to one side to make room for his elbows.

'Some things you never forget,' he said. 'It was light nights, the middle of the summer, and I'd been left with the job of locking up after two engineers who'd been on site all day working on a crane. Time? About half past nine. I can remember clocking-out and thinking the extra money from the overtime I'd done would come in handy. But just as I was putting the padlock on the gate, I noticed a van with its sidelights on stopped by the bridge.'

'What did you make of it?'

'I wasn't sure but, apart from courting couples, I couldn't see what business anybody would have coming down here just as it was getting dark. I was on my own, remember, with the keys to the yard in my pocket and some easy pickings inside for anyone looking to make a quick quid.'

'Go on.'

'I pinned my hopes on whoever was in the van not seeing me. I took no chances. I stayed in the shadows hoping they would drive off.'

'What happened?'

'At first nothing, then somebody got out of the driver's side and went round the back of the van where I couldn't see what they were doing. After what seemed like ages they appeared again and had a good look round before they got back in. Then the van did a three-point turn and drove off. It was the following day when we heard about the body of the girl being found. There were coppers everywhere, detectives in plain clothes, another lot in uniform.'

'They interviewed you?'

'They interviewed everybody.'

'You told them what you'd seen?'

'I told them what I've just told you.'

'Were you able to give them a description of the driver of the van?'

'Male, medium height, clean-shaven – he was too far away to make out his features clearly.'

'What about the van?'

'A battered old Morris J4 – grey with a big dent in the side. I didn't clock the number plate. I could have kicked myself afterwards.'

'You're saying you think you may have witnessed the girl's body being dumped?'

'The van was stopped where a path used to go down to the canal towpath. It's not there anymore. Like I said, I couldn't see what was going on because the van was in the way.'

'Coming back to when the police interviewed you, what reaction did you get when you told them what you'd seen?'

'They asked me to make a statement which I did then, later in the day, I was told a crack team of detectives was coming down from the city to take over.'

'What happened?'

'I was told somebody would get back to me but they never did. The next I heard they'd made an arrest.'

'So what made you think the police got the wrong man?'

'The man I saw was white. The bloke they arrested was black – light skinned but definitely black. His mugshot was in all the papers.'

'What some people might call a white Jamaican?'

'I suppose they might.'

'Did you raise this with anybody?'

'The detective who first interviewed me – I still had the card he'd given me with his contact details on it so I rang him up.'

'What did he have to say for himself?'

'The matter was now out of his hands.'

'Did you speak to anybody else?'

'The boss's father who was still running the place at the time.'

'And...'

'He told me to drop it – and, when I thought about it, I could see where he was coming from. Getting on the wrong side of the law doesn't pay in the scrap metal trade.'

'Tell me something,' said Moon looking round as he stood on the steps of the caravan preparing to leave. 'Am I right in thinking a place like this would be a Mecca to somebody who spends his spare time doing up classic cars? The kind of character who goes round with a set of spanners cannibalizing parts off old wrecks?'

'You could be,' said the man rubbing the growth of stubble on his chin.

'You don't seem certain.'

'Classic cars sounds more to me like cars from the fifties and sixties. Typical of what we get coming in here are the kind of cars you see every day going up and down the motorway. Accident write-offs mostly. If you're talking about cars like old E-type Jags and Austin-Healeys then you'd have to turn the clock back twenty or thirty years.'

'Thanks,' said Moon. 'That's all I wanted to know.'

'Something I didn't mention,' said the man as he walked Moon back to the gate. 'There were two people in the van – the driver, the one I told you about, and somebody else who was sitting in the passenger seat.'

'You're sure?'

'As sure as I'm standing here now having this conversation with you.'

'Did you get a look at the other person?'

The man shook his head. 'They stayed in the van – but I can tell you one thing.'

'What's that?'

'It was a woman. I'd stake my life on it.'

CHAPTER FOURTEEN

SARAH'S STORY

As he drove back into the city, Moon's thoughts turned to Christmas Day. Watching the girls open their presents. Visiting the cemetery where his parents were buried and putting a wreath on their grave. Cathy's mother coming for lunch, carving the turkey, pulling crackers and nagging the girls to eat their sprouts. This year no different to the last. A few days off to unwind if he was lucky. Time to recharge the batteries, space to get his head straight but then what? Back to the never-ending game of cat and mouse which had cast such a shadow over his life for the last two years.

• • •

'What made you go back to where Sharon's body was found?' Jo asked when he met up with her later. 'Don't tell me it was another of your hunches.'

'It isn't the kind of place anybody would come across by accident,' Moon replied. 'Unless we're barking up the wrong tree altogether there had to be a link which connected it to Morris. Some reason why he knew it.'

'The link being Morris's hobby of doing up old cars? The scrapyard being a place somebody like him would go and visit?'

'That's the theory. After he knifed Sharon he got hold of a van, put her body in the back and drove it there thinking nobody would see him. He chose a time when he thought the crew at the scrapyard would have knocked off and gone home. He knew exactly what he was doing.'

'What about the woman? Are we saying he had an accomplice?'

'It looks like it. Who? From what we know of his sexual habits, I'm sure he was well acquainted with any number of women but, when you think about it, an accomplice to murder needed to be somebody he could trust – which, in the context of Jake Morris, translates into somebody he felt he could control.'

'Didn't Duncan tell you there was a rumour Morris was two-timing Sharon?'

'Yes, he did, but, like you say, it was just a rumour.'

They were sitting in a city centre wine bar mixing with the crowds who had spilled out of nearby offices. Jo put her glass down.

'What about Sarah's sister?' she said. 'It sounds like she fits the profile of somebody Morris could rely on to do as she was told.'

Moon looked at her. 'Trish Phillips didn't say when she first met him. For all we know she may not have come onto the scene until later.'

'What about Sarah?'

'What about her?'

'She would be able to tell us.'

'You're saying we should ask Trish to set up a meeting.'

'Unless you have any better ideas. If not, I'm happy to speak to Trish.'

When Moon got back to the car after seeing Jo off he switched his phone back on and noticed a missed call from Thompson.

'Hang on a minute, Guv,' said Thompson when the line connected. Moon could hear the noise of music and laughter in the background and he guessed Thompson had stopped off at a pub on his way back home to drown his post-marital sorrows in drink. He imagined him now elbowing his way through a crowd of people looking for somewhere quieter to talk.

'Guess what?' said Thompson when he came back on the line. 'Not long after I spoke to you earlier DI Millership arrived on site. He hadn't been in for more than five minutes when he asked Tambo to go up and see him.'

'Tambo?'

'That's right. Apparently he began by asking Tambo how he was enjoying life on the Team and whether he'd given any thought to how his future might shape up. Tambo tried to play it cagey, not sure where the conversation was leading. Then DI Millership talked about how he and Mr Willoughby had been giving some thought to succession planning – identifying junior members of the Team who could be considered promotion material, the next generation of senior officers, so to speak. Not really saying anything but dropping out big hints there could be something in it for Tambo if he played ball. Guv, he was trying to recruit Tambo to spy on us. That's what Tambo thought too.'

'What did Tambo say?'

'He acted thick to the point where DI Millership realised he was flogging a dead horse and gave up. Tambo said it was like turning off a tap. One minute he was all chummy and greasy smiles; the next, he couldn't wait to get Tambo out of the door.'

• • •

Two days went by before Moon heard from Jo again. He was at his desk when he took the call and, conscious of the listening device no more than a few feet from where he was sitting, he told her he would ring back. Grabbing his overcoat, he made his way outside using the fire door as an exit to avoid passing the front desk. Two skips stood at the far end of the site where every night the office cleaners took the rubbish they'd collected from bins and waste paper baskets. A wind was getting up, blowing litter about on the car park, while dark rain clouds were gathering in the sky. Between the furthest skip and the perimeter fence was a gap where he knew from previous experience he could stand without being seen from upstairs. He checked the time. It was just after eleven.

'Charlie, I took a call from Trish Phillips earlier,' Jo said when she answered after three rings. 'The good news is Sarah is happy to meet up providing Trish is present but there's a condition. Trish wants us to promise we won't ask Sarah any questions about what happened between her and her sister. She's worried it might upset her and undo all the good work that's been done.'

'Sounds reasonable enough to me – has an arrangement been made?'

'Subject to your availability, Trish is suggesting two o'clock on Friday afternoon over at her place. We can make our ways separately just in case somebody at your end gets ideas about having you tailed. I've told Trish to tell Sarah she can trust you.'

After ending the call to Jo, Moon put his phone back in his pocket and stood for a while. In front of him, the modern red-brick building which had served as headquarters for Team Penda since its inception – a building which looked like all the others on the business park where it was located; a building he had grown to hate over the years but where, in bad moments, he could see himself serving out his time until the day he retired.

Just as he was on the point of making his way back to his office he spotted Thompson pulling onto the car park. Thompson saw him too and, after reversing into an empty space, he came across.

'Scotty, Tambo and me met up for a pint last night,' said Thompson. 'We're all worried about what DI Millership might do next. Sooner or later he'll lay a trap and one of us will fall into it.'

Moon nodded. 'I know what you're saying, Dave. Millership may be all the things we know he is but nobody can beat him when it comes to dirty tricks. He knows too this is his big chance to shine in Mr Willoughby's eyes. He'll stoop as low as he can go to find something to pin on me – something the two of them can get their teeth in. Time's not on our side.'

• • •

When Friday came round Moon took the precaution of booking the afternoon off using the pretext of going Christmas shopping. Over the course of the morning he caught occasional glimpses of Millership without coming face to face with him. Willoughby was on site somewhere – holed up in his office, Moon guessed.

He drove off the car park at twenty past twelve making his first port of call the sandwich shop where he bought a cheese salad baguette. As he left the sandwich shop he did a careful check in his mirrors to make sure nobody was following. His plan was to drive to where Trish Phillips lived by keeping off main roads and avoiding places where police CCTV cameras watched over everything. He realised he was probably being overcautious but, as he knew full well, it was no use being sorry if reports filtered back to Willoughby afterwards that he'd been seen heading off in the opposite direction to the shops.

Eating the baguette as he drove along, he soon left the busy streets behind. He had plenty of time so he didn't hurry. He chose quiet country roads with long straight stretches which had once echoed to the tramp of Roman legions and where he could look back half a mile to make sure nobody was following. Over hill and down dale he slowly started to unwind. He put a CD in the CD player. He saw how tassels of Traveller's Joy hung over the hedgerows while the low sun picked out the colours of the last few leaves left on the trees. Flocks of fieldfares and redwings flew off as he approached while a solitary stoat stopped to stare as it crossed the road before vanishing into a ditch.

He came to a meeting of ways where he went left ignoring a sign to say there was no through road. Soon he was back on familiar territory – the sunken lane with tall banks on either side which he knew would take him down to the river. A mile further on he drew up next to the field of stubble where a few more cars were parked than last time including, he noticed, Jo's little Fiat.

As he got out of the car and stretched his legs, he stood for a few moments to take in his surroundings. A wooden pallet was propped up against the hedge which hadn't been there before while the chugging of a tractor at work somewhere reached his ears. He took the narrow path again already deep in shadow and soon he heard the sound of the river up in front. Twenty yards further on, he got his first glimpse of it through the trees. The swirling water was higher, the fallen elm almost totally submerged, and, on the far bank, he could see cattle grazing in a waterlogged meadow. He came to the bridge over the brook with its slippery planks and its rickety handrail reminding him he'd forgotten again to change out of his city shoes. The brook was in full spate, cascading down towards the river and making a wild noise as it plunged from pool to pool over weirs of silt and fallen twigs. The white gate stood open and the way into the terraced garden where he saw once more the long flight of steps leading up to the white-walled cottage at the top.

'Hi.'

He recognised Trish Phillips' cheerful voice straight away. She was standing at the cottage door looking out for him.

'Everyone else arrived early,' she said taking his overcoat from him after he'd wiped his feet on the coconut mat. She then led him, not through to the kitchen this time, but into a low-ceilinged room where Jo was waiting to greet him. Next to her stood a middle-aged woman with delicate porcelain features and dark shoulder-length hair.

'This is Sarah,' said Jo moving to one side to allow Moon space to come across and shake hands.

'Shall we sit down?' said Trish pointing to three sofas grouped around a log fire burning in a large open grate. 'I've put some coffee on and it should be ready in a few minutes.'

Moon took in more details of the room. Lattice windows on two sides, a vase of flowers on a small table over in a corner, books on bookshelves next to the chimney breast. He imagined it to be where Trish did her counselling. A tranquil place away from the hustle and bustle of everyday life with just the hissing of the logs burning in the grate and the noise of the brook coming from outside. Jo had taken a seat next to Sarah on the furthest of the sofas while Moon sat down on the one by the door. Jo was first to speak.

'I've explained to Sarah why you want to talk to her,' she said to him. 'I'll leave the rest to you.'

Moon switched his attention to Sarah. She was sitting on the edge of the sofa with her hands clasped around her knees.

Taking the cue from Jo, Moon went over the story of the man and woman who were seen behaving suspiciously in the vicinity of where Sharon Baxter's body was later found. 'It could be a red herring,' he said. 'But, because we don't have a lot else to go on, we need to check it out.'

'You're saying the woman could have been my sister?' said Sarah speaking for the first time.

'I'm saying we can't afford to leave any stone unturned. We need a breakthrough and, unless we get one soon, we could be about to witness Morris slipping through our fingers.'

'I gather you want to know when Tess – my sister – started going out with him? The answer is May 1975.'

'You seem very certain of the date.'

'It was just after her twenty-first birthday. She met him at a club.'

'Which seems to confirm what we thought. Morris was carrying on with Sharon and your sister at the same time. Does that surprise you?'

'I can't say it does. There were always rumours about him being seen out with other girls.'

'What about your sister? Did she suspect he was two-timing her?'

'If she did she never said anything to me. Not that she would have ever spoken a bad word against him. Whatever he did, she always stood by him.'

'Would that include helping cover up a murder? Going along on the night he drove through the streets of the city with Sharon's body in the back of a van then acting as a lookout for him? Swallowing whatever cock and bull story he gave her for what he was doing with the corpse of a girl on his hands?'

'When it came to protecting him, I have to say nothing would shock me.'

'I'll fetch the coffee,' said Trish sensing the pause in the conversation. While she was out of the room nobody spoke. The smoke from the fire twisted and curled as it went up the chimney. Finally she came back in carrying a tray filled with cups.

Moon waited for Trish to finish handing the coffee round before he turned to Sarah again. 'Let me put another question to you,' he said. 'We know Morris had a history of violence when it came to asserting his authority over women. What can you tell us about the way he treated your sister? I ask because being scared of what he might do to her could point to why she chose to help him. Did he threaten her? Did she toe the line because she was too frightened to do otherwise? Or was there more to it? Something we haven't considered?'

'It was never plain to me what Tess saw in him,' Sarah replied.

'But what?'

'Going back to before she met him she always wanted the big house in the country, the children who took riding lessons and went to private schools. She had it fixed in her head she was cut out for better things and perhaps that's what drew her to him. Somebody who had the same ideas and, if you're looking for a reason why she turned a blind eye to the side of him everybody else hated, that could be it. In the end I came to the conclusion they were made for one another. '

'It's often the case with abused women,' said Trish as she went round the room switching on table lamps. 'They're in love with the monsters who mistreat them. They become victims of their own emotions. Sadly I've seen it many times. They end up in a trap from which there's no escape.'

'She wanted children?' This came from Jo who hadn't taken her eyes off Sarah all the time she'd been talking. Sarah didn't answer. She stared into the fire watching the flames flicker.

Moon spoke again. 'We can understand why you don't want to talk about events you find upsetting,' he said. 'At the same time we're trying to put together a picture of your sister from a lot of jumbled fragments so is there any more you can tell us? About your sister? About what might explain how she could have become an accomplice to murder?'

'She wasn't all bad. She may have done her best to hide it but there was good in her somewhere. No, that's not me sticking up for her because she's my sister. I hoped one day she would grow up and come to her senses but she didn't. She met Morris and, after that, she chose her own path. I wish it was different but that's the way it is.'

'I'm guessing there's more,' said Moon.

'There's much more,' Sarah replied.

CHAPTER FIFTEEN

COLD HOUSE, COLD HEARTS

Sarah was stopping the night with Trish to avoid driving home in the dark. She stayed behind in the cottage while Trish walked Jo and Moon back to their cars using a torch to light the way. A few stars were out in the sky and a mist was rising up off the river.

'You'll keep in touch?' said Trish when they arrived at the field of stubble.

'Yes, of course,' said Moon.

Trish turned to Jo. 'We must meet up in the New Year. I'd like to hear more about the articles you're writing.'

'I look forward to it,' said Jo.

Jo and Moon watched her as she set off down the narrow track with the earthy smells. The light of her torch gradually drew further and further away until finally it vanished. They stood for a while, breathing in the cold night air and listening to the sounds that reached their ears. A roosting pheasant, three short barks of a dog fox, sheep settling down in the field.

'Correct me if I'm wrong,' said Jo as she tightened the knot in her scarf. 'We came today hoping to shed some light on what happened back in 1978 but we seem to have ended up with more questions than we started with.'

'I agree,' said Moon turning to face her. 'If Sarah's sister was the mystery woman who was seen with Morris on the night he disposed of Sharon's body I still can't figure out what she was doing there. Short of a complete mental blackout who in their right mind would allow themselves to be sucked into a scheme to pin a murder on an innocent man? OK, I accept she may have been besotted with Morris and, for that reason, not acting rationally but surely some alarm bells would have been going off in her head. To top it all the body she helped him to dump belonged to a girl he'd been sleeping with – which brings me to number two. Why, we have to ask ourselves, did Morris involve her in the first place? Even if he felt confident he could rely on her to do as she was told, surely he would have been doing all he could to stop her finding out what he'd been getting up to behind her back.'

'Is there a number three?'

'Yes there is. I listened to what Sarah had to say about Tess's craving for material things but I still don't understand why she stayed with him. A self-confessed murderer, a bully, a philanderer who went round getting young girls pregnant – is this the kind of person anybody in their right mind would want to spend the rest of their life with? The more I think about it, the less sense it makes.

It makes even less sense when you factor in what Andy Woodall told us. In 1975 when Tess started going out with him, Morris was still grooming little kids which begs the question what did she know? If she was aware of the depths of his depravity what on earth was she doing getting married to him? A woman who wanted children doesn't fit the profile of somebody who would condone luring young lads into the clutches of perverts like Sid Marples.'

Jo frowned. 'So what are you saying, Charlie? We've got this wrong?'

'I'm saying, apart from Jake Morris, only one person has the answer.'

'You mean Tess?'

Moon walked with her across to where the little Fiat was parked. 'What are you doing on Monday?' he said as he held the door open for her to get in.

'That sounds suspiciously like an invitation to join you on one of your mystery excursions. Roping me in on a game of good cop, bad cop played to your version of the rules. I've been there before, remember. I've done it and got the tee shirt.'

'So?'

'I've got articles to write, deadlines to meet before Christmas. Before I go blindly agreeing to anything, can you tell me exactly what it is you've got in mind?'

'Tess, Sarah's sister – I thought we might go and pay her a visit.'

'The idea being what?'

'To see what she has to say for herself if she thinks the game's up.'

'You're suggesting we bluff her into believing we've built a case against Morris when we haven't? What if she doesn't buy it?

'That's the risk we take. The downside is me finishing up in front of Willoughby explaining what I was doing harassing the wife of a respectable local businessman.'

'What's the upside?'

'She spills the beans. We get the breakthrough we need, Wilson Beames' conviction is overturned, Morris goes to jail.'

• • •

It was just after nine on Monday morning when Moon picked Jo up from her apartment. They drove first to the offices of JCM Litigation where Moon pointed to the green MGB parked outside. It meant Jake Morris was busy at his desk and the coast was clear for catching his wife at home on her own.

When they reached the house set back from the lane Moon pulled up on the grass verge. Getting out into the cold, he retrieved his overcoat from the back seat while Jo did her best to stop her heels sinking in the mud. A paved path led off the drive to the front door where Moon pressed the bell and waited for somebody to come. Presently a woman appeared who bore a faint resemblance to Sarah although nobody seeing them side by side would have guessed they were sisters. She wore a grey trouser suit but whether she was the same woman Moon had seen standing out in the cold a week ago was impossible to say.

She opened the door cautiously, taking the chain off only when she'd looked Jo and Moon up and down a few times.

Moon spoke. 'I'm Detective Inspector Moon,' he said holding up his ID. 'This is Ms Lyon who is assisting me with some inquiries. Can we have a word please?'

The woman moved to one side to let them in. Once they were through the door she closed it and put the chain back on.

'This may be better sitting down,' said Moon feeling the need to say something because the woman still stood there with a blank expression on her face. The suggestion seemed to take a few seconds to register but finally she led them off along a hallway with a parquet floor which echoed to their footsteps. They went through into a small sitting room where two green leather sofas were positioned in front of an empty fireplace with a coffee table taking up the space between them. Moon shivered. Either the central heating wasn't programmed to be on at this time of day or, if it was, the radiators were turned down to their lowest setting. Cold house, cold hearts: it had been one of his mother's favourite sayings. He took a seat on one of the sofas while Jo did the same. At first it looked like the woman was going to remain standing but, after a few seconds, she came and sat down opposite them giving Moon a chance to study her face. Like Sarah, fine features, prominent cheekbones: she may have been pretty once but time had taken its toll.

Moon cleared his throat. ' We're here in connection with a crime committed twenty-three years ago. A student named Sharon Baxter was stabbed to death and her body left at the side of a canal. We believe you may know something about it. We're acting on information which has come to light recently.'

'I don't have a clue what you're talking about.' It was the first time she'd spoken and Moon noticed the colour starting to rise in her cheeks.

'Don't you? Come off it, Mrs Morris. Your husband had a relationship with Miss Baxter, didn't he? She was a pretty young girl with a bright future and she ended up dead.'

'I've told you I don't know anything. If this is to do with my husband you'll have to speak to him.'

'Can't you see we're giving you a chance? Your husband is going to go to prison and, unless you play your cards right, you'll be joining him. Conspiracy to pervert the course of justice; assisting an offender – serious crimes calling for long sentences. You could finish up spending years behind bars. So don't try telling us you know nothing because it won't wash. You were seen with him on the night he took Miss Baxter's body to the place where it was later found. You were there and you saw everything that happened so the sooner you come clean about what you know, the better it will be for you.'

'People have always had it in for him,' she blazed backed angrily. 'You're no different to all the rest. Believe what these liars have told you.'

'In which case let's continue,' said Moon. 'We've been investigating allegations against senior police officers who were known to have connections with your husband and who may have helped him conceal his involvement in a range of criminal activities not just Miss Baxter's murder.

We want you tell us what you know about his dealings with the police – dates, identities, who gave him money, who wasn't above doing him a good turn.'

'My husband is a businessman. He keeps his affairs to himself.'

'Stop trying to pull the wool over our eyes Mrs Morris. You've known him for twenty-five years, lived with him during most of that time. You must have seen what went on. Don't waste our time pretending you didn't.'

'If you're suggesting my husband is a criminal you're mistaken. He's worked hard all his life. Never done anything wrong. Now, can I ask you to leave? Whoever has made these accusations isn't telling you the truth. They're the ones who should be going to prison, not him.'

• • •

'So much for me and my big ideas,' said Moon when Jo and he got back to the car.

Jo smiled. 'Don't take it to heart,' she said. 'What you saw there was years of conditioning which nothing you or I said was going to penetrate. She's hiding something but she won't give up her secrets easily.'

Moon looked out of the window to where dark clouds were starting to gather in the sky over in the distance. 'The clock's ticking,' he said glumly. 'I need to get to the bottom of this before Willoughby and Millership come up with a new plan for taking me down. Now, to add to our problems, we've got the prospect of Mrs Morris getting on the phone to her husband and telling him what just happened. For all

I know he could still have friends in high places and my days could already be numbered. Look at what happened to Alf Stepney. I could be next on the list.'

• • •

Moon dropped Jo off in the city centre where she had another appointment. He checked the time. It was just after twelve. He pulled into a meter bay where he sat with the engine running while he made a call to Thompson.

'Still all quiet,' said Thompson. 'Too quiet to my way of thinking.'

'Dave, do me a favour. I may not be in for a while. Hold the fort, will you?'

'Sure Guv but what do you want me to say if someone from upstairs starts asking questions about where you are?'

'Tell them I've got the flu. Lay it on thick if you have to.'

• • •

Snow started to fall as he drove home later. Small flurries at first then large flakes as the streetlights started to come on. He'd spent the afternoon browsing in charity shops looking at vinyls and CDs for anything that caught his eye. The fruits of his labours included a compilation of rare recordings from the twenties and thirties, many of which he'd never heard before. It made him think of Jo as he played one of the tracks and it was a coincidence she rang just as it finished.

'Charlie.' He pressed the eject button of the CD player and put Jo on hands-free so he could listen to what she had to say. 'Trish Phillips rang about half an hour ago to say she'd just taken a call from Sarah who sounded shaken and upset. It seems Sarah only works half a day on Mondays and, not long after she got back home earlier, the phone rang but, when she picked it up, there was nobody there. Not thinking anything to it, she put the handset back down but, minutes later, it rang again and again it was the same – nobody there. When this had happened a few more times Sarah started to think it was a nuisance caller – some crank who'd got hold of her ex-directory number and was trying to scare her. In the end, though, she thought to dial 1471 and guess what? The number that came up was one she recognised straight away. Tess. Tess who she hadn't spoken to for years.'

'What did Sarah do?'

'The next time the phone rang she didn't answer. After that the calls stopped.'

'Did you tell Trish we'd been to see Tess this morning?'

'I told her everything. I thought she had a right to know.'

'What did she say?'

'She thought we may have unleashed something – something Tess couldn't handle. She turned to Sarah because she felt she had no one else she could talk to but in the end words failed her.'

• • •

It was early the following afternoon when Moon took the call from Andy Woodall.

'I don't want to talk over the phone,' he said and they agreed to meet at a roadhouse on the outskirts of town which was a well-known gathering place for bikers. There had been more snow in the night leaving a covering of two or three inches on the ground.

It took Moon less time than he expected to drive to the roadhouse. He took care as he pulled onto the front which served as a car park knowing the compacted snow could be concealing all manner of ruts and potholes. He counted four trucks and a van outside while a sign advertising all-day breakfasts lay on the ground where it had either been blown over in the night or succumbed to some other mishap. Getting out of the car he felt the cold air on his cheeks and through his shirtsleeves prompting him to go round to the boot where he kept the all-weather high-vis jacket which was part of his standard kit. He checked his watch. He was still early and so he stood watching the traffic go by while, a few yards away, a robin picked at a brown paper bag somebody had dropped.

He didn't have long to wait. The motorbike appeared with the familiar figure in leathers sitting astride it gripping the handlebars tightly because of the fear of skidding on a patch of ice. It drew up not far from where Moon was standing and, once the engine had been switched off, he watched as Andy removed his crash helmet.

'Shall we grab a cuppa?' Moon said pointing over in the direction of the roadhouse.

Andy nodded and together they walked across to the entrance where, once inside, Moon noticed the smell of fry-ups and stale cigarettes. Trade looked like it was slack at this hour, the only other customers being a few men sitting at tables on their own reading redtops and tucking into plates of bacon, eggs and sausages. A television tuned in to a daytime chat show was fixed to one wall but nobody appeared to be watching it.

Moon paid for two large mugs of strong truck drivers' tea at the self-service counter and carried them across to where Andy had taken a seat next to a window overlooking the car park.

'I expect you're wondering what this is about,' Andy began as he took the mug from Moon and clutched it tightly in both hands. 'It may surprise you to hear this but I saw you yesterday when you and your colleague called on Morris's wife. I was up in the same place where you found me the other day. I'd been there since dawn because I don't work on Sunday nights. I watched you go in and I watched you come out. I knew Morris's wife was on her own because I'd seen him go off earlier.'

'And what?'

'I could say I acted on impulse but I wouldn't be telling the truth. Ever since I heard the story of what really happened to Liz, I've been racking my brains trying to think how to make Morris pay for what he did to her and what he did to me. Like I said when we met last time, it would have been the easiest thing in the world to drag him up a dark alley one night and beat the shit out of him but, when I thought it through properly, I saw any feeling of satisfaction would have been short-lived. After the cuts and bruises healed he would have gone back to living the life of Riley in his big posh house while I carried on toiling at my bench night after night.'

'You came up with a better plan?'

'Something that's been going through my mind for a while. When the time was right I was going to tell his wife what he did to me, every little detail, and, once she heard the truth about what he got up to all those years ago, I'd see how long it took for his world to start falling apart. You could say I banked everything on her not knowing how he targeted kids like me. I had it all worked out what I was going to say. I was going to pick the right moment but you showing up yesterday changed everything. You see, Inspector, you putting him behind bars for some other crime he's committed won't help me lay my ghosts to rest and that's where you and me are different. You're a policeman doing your duty, a job you're paid to do, but what's between me and Morris is personal. You've heard my story and you know how, thanks to him, I was left with nothing and that's why I want him to suffer in a way which would make us even. I wanted to see his life ruined, his reputation torn to shreds, and – who knows – even to make his wife think about walking out on him.'

'So you decided to get in first? You went to see her before I had a chance to lead him away in handcuffs? Was that the idea?'

Andy didn't answer. He stared out of the window at where a gritting truck was using the roadhouse car park to turn round.

Moon spoke again. 'What did you do? Wait for us to leave then go up to the front door and ring the bell?'

'Once I'd plucked up the courage.'

'Tell me what happened?'

'The words didn't come out in the way I planned but I told her the whole story. Everything.'

'How did she take it?'

'At first I wasn't sure. I realised how I must have looked to her dressed in leathers but then I started crying. I couldn't help myself. I stood there, a grown man sobbing like a little child. I told her about the way he'd fooled me into thinking he was my friend when he wasn't.'

'Do you think she knew about him?'

'It's hard to say. She gave away nothing.'

'But what?'

'I've spent my life bottling up the secret of what happened to me all those years ago and I know what it feels like to be haunted by demons from the past. As she stood there listening to me that's what I saw in her eyes. A victim. Somebody who knows suffering. A sad person who gets by somehow but for who bad memories are always there and never go away.'

'Why are you telling me this?'

'I didn't know what to do. I thought about it at work last night. The way I saw it was you've played fair with me and I reckoned I owed it to you to play fair in return. I went yesterday on a mission to get my own back but I came away not knowing what to think. Something inside her crumbled. In the end I could see she was struggling to choke back the tears.'

• • •

Moon watched Andy ride off the roadhouse car park and join the line of traffic on the main road. It was already starting to get dark. Cars and buses had their headlights on and the sky overhead told of more snow on the way. When he got back into the car he made it his first job to ring Jo.

'So what we're looking at is the phone calls Sarah received from Tess would have been made after Andy Woodall went to see her,' said Moon after filling Jo in.

'What do you think it could mean?' said Jo sounding puzzled.

'Search me, Jo, but one thing's for sure. We need to go and pay Tess another visit.'

CHAPTER SIXTEEN

THE FINAL STRAW

After speaking to Jo, his first thought was to ring Cathy to let her know he was going to be late. The line, however, went straight onto voicemail then he remembered Cathy was taking the girls out late night Christmas shopping and he'd been left with the job of getting his own dinner.

The snow started to fall again as he made his way back into the city whipped up by a wind which quickly turned into a blizzard. Windscreen wipers thrashing, he concentrated on keeping a safe distance from cars in front. He picked Jo up where he'd dropped her off the day before. Neither of them spoke as they drove out of the centre and through the suburbs. They passed a road traffic accident where an ambulance with blue lights flashing was on the scene watched by a crowd of onlookers from nearby houses who'd braved the weather to come and stare. They came to where the streetlights ended and out into open country with snow driving across the carriageway sideways and piling into drifts against the hedgerows. He picked out the turning to the left where the tracks of a few cars showed somebody had gone that way since the snow started. He kept in second gear. The lane hadn't been treated and he knew there were deep ditches on either side while the blizzard was fast becoming a white-out. He knew it couldn't be much further but it was Jo who was first to see the lights in front. When Moon pulled up he stopped far enough onto the verge to leave room for any passers-by. Out of the warmth of the car, they were aware at once of the biting cold and the sting of swirling snow driving into their faces.

Powerful halogen lamps lit the front of the house showing the path that led to the front door covered in a deep layer of fresh snow. Half way along the path Moon felt a tug on his sleeve. He turned to see Jo looking then saw what she'd seen. Over on the far side of the drive a car had been left half in and half out of the circle of light cast by the bright lamps. The unmistakable shape of a 1960s MGB with snow on the roof and snow on the bonnet showing it had been there since before the blizzard started.

'What now?' said Jo.

'We'll take it as it comes,' Moon replied. 'If Morris is around we'll deal with him. Trust me.'

When they arrived at the front door an unexpected sight met their eyes. It was standing open – just far enough to let a fine powder of snow drift over the doorstep and settle on the parquet floor inside. Moon looked round, automatically searching for signs of forced entry but finding none. He put his finger on the doorbell and pressed – once, twice, three times.

'Looks like nobody's in,' Jo whispered from where she was standing close behind.

Moon said nothing. He pushed the door gently, letting it go back on its hinges so he could see further along the hallway with its bare plaster walls lit dimly by a single glass chandelier hanging from the ceiling. Treading warily he went in front while Jo followed. The first door they came to turned out to be a cloakroom: a wash-hand basin with a gilt-framed mirror, a towel on a towel rail and a row of empty coat hooks on the wall. They went on, coming next to the small sitting room and this was where they found her. She was sitting on one of the green leather sofas with a smile on her face and seemingly lost in a world of her own. She was wearing the same grey trouser suit she'd worn the day before, sitting with one hand resting on top of the other, an empty glass on the coffee table in front of her with what looked like dregs of red wine in the bottom. She didn't look up as Moon took a seat on the other sofa so he was facing her. Jo, meanwhile, stayed by the door.

Moon spoke softly. 'Can we talk?' he said.

She looked at him: a faraway thoughtful look.

'Sharon Baxter,' Moon prompted. 'When we came to see you yesterday we asked you to tell us what you knew about her death. We wanted to know if it was you who helped your husband dispose of her body. We're talking about the summer of 1978. One night just as it was getting dark two people, a man and a woman, were seen acting suspiciously close to where she was later found covered in stab wounds.'

He watched as she slowly brought her eyes into focus.

'Let's take this from the beginning,' Moon continued. 'When did you first learn the man you'd put so much faith in had been carrying on with somebody else? Did he tell you? Did he come clean about what he'd been getting up to?'

There was a long pause before she answered. 'It was one afternoon,' she said finally in a voice scarcely more than a whisper. 'I went round to his flat expecting to find him there but when nobody came to the door, I let myself in.'

'You had a key?'

She shook her head. 'No, but I knew where he kept a spare hanging on a piece of string inside the letter box.'

'Go on.'

'As usual the place was a tip so I decided to pass the time while I was waiting tidying up and putting things away. That's when I came across a folder with her name on it. She must have left it there.'

'What was in the folder?'

'College work, essays, that sort of stuff. That's how I found out she was a student. But then I found something else. The report of a pregnancy test she'd had done. I felt sick after I read it. I knew it was him.'

'Then what?'

'I went round to his flat again the next day hoping I'd catch the two of them together but it was just her on her own. She was lying on the bed asleep. The knife was out of the kitchen drawer. All I can remember was the blood. It was everywhere and the knife was in my hand. I can't say when he came back. I just remember him being there.'

'You're saying you killed Sharon not him? Is that the story you're expecting us to believe? You, the person who has spent her life protecting him, and now here you are again trying to take the rap for what he did. Come off it, Mrs Morris.'

'What I'm telling you is the truth. When he saw what I'd done he panicked. After he calmed down he said we needed to move the body to a place where it wouldn't be discovered for a few days. He told me he wanted time to sort things out. He had a mate with a van he could borrow. He told me everything would be all right as long as I kept my mouth shut.'

'Go on.'

'I helped him wrap the body in an old duvet. He rented a garage nearby and we left it there while he went to fetch the van. While he was gone I did my best to clean up the blood. We got rid of the mattress and the carpet later. We took them to a place down a farm track used by fly-tippers where we soaked them in petrol and put a match to them. Later we did the same with our clothes.'

'What happened to the knife?'

'He took care of it.'

'What I don't get is why, when you found out Morris was playing around behind your back, you didn't just walk away and leave him to sort out his own mess. If this story you're telling us is true I don't understand why you felt you had to kill Sharon. Are you saying you acted in a fit of jealous rage or was there more to it?'

A clock chimed somewhere. The curtains were caught in a draught from the door.

'Why did I do what I did?' she said after the silence had gone on for a while. 'It goes back to the summer of 1976 when I'd been going out with him for about a year. I discovered I was pregnant. When I told him the news I expected him to say we'd get married. We both had savings. There seemed to be no reason why we couldn't.'

'Are you telling me he had different ideas?'

'He said he wasn't ready to start thinking about settling down and taking on responsibilities. He made it clear he didn't want the baby. He wanted me to go and have an abortion.'

'What about you? What did you think?'

'The idea of it cut me to the core. I'd always wanted children.'

'And Morris – what did he do when it came to respecting your wishes?'

'He was adamant about me having the abortion. He made it plain I was on my own if I didn't do something. To this day I can still hear his voice. Cold and heartless. I should have known then he didn't really love me.'

'I take it you gave in to him. You had the abortion. You put your own feelings to one side rather than run the risk of him going off and leaving you.'

'I went to a private clinic. He took me in his car and left me there. He wanted to pay for everything but I wouldn't let me there. He wanted to pay for everything but I wouldn't let him. It was August. The weather was hot, the way it had been all summer. It was a day I'll never forget for as long as I live.'

'So Morris had his way. The pregnancy was stopped and he no longer had to worry about being lumbered with a child he didn't want.'

'He bought me a gold bracelet and gave it to me on the morning he picked me up from the clinic. He told me it was my present for having the abortion. I never wore it. It's still at the back of a drawer upstairs.'

'Did anybody else know about you being pregnant?'

For a moment it looked like she might burst into tears but the moment passed.

'I didn't want to tell my sister Sarah because I felt so ashamed but she could see I'd been crying and she kept asking me what was wrong. At first I wouldn't I tell her but, in the end, she guessed.'

'You told her about Morris pushing you into having an abortion.'

'She could see how devastated I was and she said I didn't have to go through with it if I didn't want to. She told me she would do everything she could to help.'

'Yet you still had the abortion. You did what Morris wanted you to do. What did Sarah think? '

'She couldn't believe it especially when I went on seeing him.'

'She must have found that difficult.'

'She still did her best to support me but I was so full of anger I made the mistake of taking the anger out on her not him. I told her it was her fault for not stepping in and stopping me having the abortion. I made her the scapegoat and, Sarah being Sarah, she soaked it all up until there was no room left inside her to soak up any more. Yes, I know it sounds like a poor excuse but I never meant to hurt her. Still I did what I did. I stood by and watched her slowly fall apart. Looking back, I should have told her I was sorry but my foolish pride wouldn't let me. I lost the best friend I ever had. I can see it clearly now. It was all my fault.'

'You never had children,' said Jo coming across. 'The dream you once had was never fulfilled.'

'It wasn't to be. The years went by and I became the sad and lonely woman you see before you today. I took it as judgment on me for what I'd done.'

Moon spoke again. 'Let me get this straight,' he said. 'You're telling us you killed Sharon when you found out she was pregnant with Morris's child. You did what you did because you wanted to make sure her baby met the same fate as yours. You saw it as your way of exacting retribution for what was done to you two years earlier but there was a catch, wasn't there? The secret you now shared with Morris trapped you into a cold and empty relationship. You married him for the sake of appearances but, as time went by, the material trappings of a big house and everything money could buy no longer offered the distraction they once did and the loathing you felt for him festered in their place. But what I don't get is why you have now decided to tell the truth about what happened all those years ago. Has your conscience finally got the better of you for standing back and letting an innocent man go to prison for the crime you committed? Or does it have something to do with the poor soul who spoke to you yesterday and told you his story? Did you see at last the depravity you'd fostered by the game of pretence you played? Didn't you know your husband preyed on children and, when you found out, was it the final straw?'

She looked at him and then rose to her feet, a little unsteadily at first. For a split second she seemed to hesitate then she led them out of the room back into the hallway with its hollow echoes. The front door was still open, the snow still blowing in. Outside, the strength of the blizzard met them head on. They followed her, a pathetic figure in her grey trouser suit with nothing on her feet except a pair of slippers. There was no mistaking the direction in which she was heading. Towards the little two-seater now completely covered in a thick blanket of snow standing on the edge of the pool of light from the halogen lamps. When she reached it, she stopped.

'Last night I waited for him to come back from work,' she said. 'He didn't come into the house straight away and, when I went outside, I saw he was sitting in his car with the door open speaking to somebody on the phone.'

Moon looked at her, the flakes of snow on her face and eyelashes and settling on her clothes and in her hair. Using his bare hands he scraped the snow from the car windscreen and there, slumped over onto the passenger side, he saw the body of a man with what looked like a gunshot wound just beneath his temple.

She spoke again. 'The gun was his,' she said. 'He kept it in the house fully loaded and taught me how to use it. He always said being in business meant he'd made a few enemies over the years. You'll find it in the bushes where I threw it.' She turned to Jo. 'Give Sarah a message from me, will you? Tell her what I've done. Only she will truly understand.'

With that, she turned and walked back towards the house. Soon there was nothing left but a trail of footprints.

POSTLUDE

When the case came to court, Tess Morris pleaded guilty to the murder of her husband. She also pleaded guilty to the murder of Sharon Baxter in 1978 and to counts of perverting the course of justice. She said little at her trial and sat calmly when the judge handed down a life sentence.

The gun she used to kill her husband was recovered from the scene of the crime and presented in evidence. It was determined by the forensics team that three shots had been fired. The first entered the victim's brain and was, without doubt, the cause of his death. The second passed through the soft tissue of his shoulder while the third missed and left a hole in the upholstery of the car in which his body was found.

Subsequently the conviction of Wilson Beames was quashed following which Detective Inspector Moon received a letter of thanks from inmates of Winson Green Prison.

In later years Duncan Toogood became headmaster of the comprehensive school where he teaches. He never married.

Jim Baxter moved to a small cottage in the rolling hills of the Peak District where he made new friends and where he still lives quietly to this day.

Charlie Moon returned to work after the Christmas break. One of his first jobs was to remove the listening device from his office. It was later found in a plain paper bag left at the front desk of Team Penda marked for the personal attention of Detective Inspector Millership.

Andy Woodall still works in the factory where he has worked for many years. The last anybody heard of him he was studying for an Open University degree in Mechanical Engineering. He hopes to graduate next year.